The Awasthis of Aamnagri

Shubha Sarma

olive turtle

NIYOGI BOOKS

Published by
NIYOGI BOOKS
Block D, Building No. 77,
Okhla Industrial Area, Phase-I,
New Delhi-110 020, INDIA
Tel: 91-11-26816301, 26818960
Email: niyogibooks@gmail.com
Website: www.niyogibooksindia.com

Editor: Arkaprabha Biswas
Cover desigh: Misha Oberoi
Layout: Shashi Bhushan Prasad

ISBN: 978-93-89136-71-5
Publication: 2020

Printed at: Niyogi Offset Pvt. Ltd., New Delhi, India

To my Mother,
the pillar of strength in my life

Prologue

'Happy families are all alike; every unhappy family is unhappy in its own way.'

—Leo Tolstoy, *Anna Karenina*

This is the story of the Awasthi family and their brick-coloured mansion named, 'Paradise'. Its high-ceilinged rooms witness drama and theatrics with a touch of mystery, where the legal luminaries of the family match their wits against each other and win many a battle against destiny. It is a tale of ghosts walking on soundless feet and parrots who talk of stolen heirlooms, of silk saris and gold necklaces and of birds flying back to their nests. But I am rushing ahead without making any sense. So, let me start from the beginning.

The story is set in Aamnagri, the city of the Emperor of all fruits—the land of luscious mangoes—where the unsullied waters of Ganga and Yamuna mingle. Occasionally, there is a glimpse of Bageechabad, also famous for its mango groves. Like every city, Aamnagri has its Station Road, the main avenue leading to the railway station. 'Paradise' was an important landmark on this road for passers-by who knew it, more commonly, as 'Pandit ji's Haveli'. It is home to Pandit Dinanath Awasthi and his brood of seven children, twelve grand-children, four pets and countless residents of the human and faunal variety. The narrative traverses several decades, charting the lives of the Awasthis and providing glimpses of a bygone era—when lazy summer vacations were spent at grandparents' homes, when families lived under one roof: fighting, bickering and in the process, rediscovering their affection for each other.

List of Characters

Pandit Dinanath Awasthi is a prominent lawyer of Aamnagri. A father figure of the family who guides his flock, he is never a typical chauvinist.

Mrs Shakuntala Awasthi is thc domineering matriarch. Without her permission, nothing stirs in the 'Paradise', yet she is often checkmated by circumstances.

Sumeet, Randheer, Sudheer and **Vineet** are the four Awasthi boys. While Sudheer is serving in the Indian Army, the others are lawyers, working with their father.

Chhaya, Varsha, Indu and **Madhu** are married to the Awasthi brothers repectively.

Kusum (Sumi), Vinodini (Vinu) and **Anamika (Anu)** are the three daughters who are the apples of their parents' eyes. Though they do not live at Aamnagri, they visit the Haveli every year during the school holidays.

Chikoo, Guddu, Pinki, Rani, Sonu and Monu are some of the half a dozen grandchildren who add a unique flavour to the multi-hued Awasthi family.

Ashok or **Chhote Mama** or **Chhote Bhaiyya** is Mrs Awasthi's younger brother. He owns a couple of mango orchards in Bageechabad. He is her prime confidante and partner in crime. His wife, Malati, is a recluse and does not mingle much with Pandit ji's family.

Chedilal, Gauri, Maharani, Gangu ***Mali*****, Lakshmi** and **Sunder** are the retainers of the Awasthi household. Their lives are inextricably intertwined with those of the Awasthis.

Munshi Shyamlal is Pandit ji's legal assistant and doubles up as his man Friday.

Babu Rameshwar Prasad is Pandit Awasthi's bosom pal. He visits them along with his son, Rohit, daughter-in-law, Seema and grandson, Kony.

Mr Saxena & Mrs Rama Saxena, Mr Singh and Mr Tiwari are friends of the Awasthis.

Mrs Lily Verma is Mrs Saxena's sister.

Vinod is Pinki's fiancé. Mr Kanhaiyya Lal Pandey and Sunita are his parents.

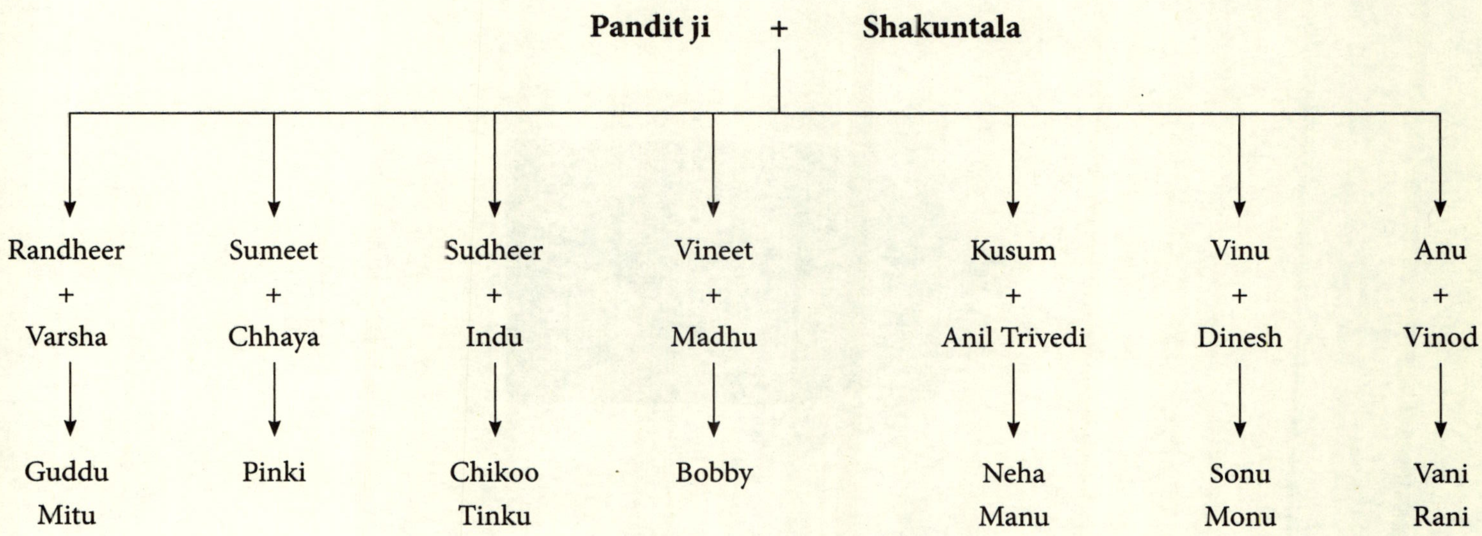
Pandit ji + Shakuntala
Randheer
+
Varsha
Guddu
Mitu
Sumeet
+
Chhaya
Pinki
Sudheer
+
Indu
Chikoo
Tinku
Vineet
+
Madhu
Bobby
Kusum
+
Anil Trivedi
Neha
Manu
Vinu
+
Dinesh
Sonu
Monu
Anu
+
Vinod
Vani
Rani

A HOUSE IS BOUGHT – A HOME IS MADE

'You call this *Paradise*?'

'*Paradise*'? Pandit Dinanath Awasthi repeated incredulously. 'Only a fool could have named this "Paradise". Or someone who was blind! Seriously, Munshi, nothing could be further drawn from the truth. *Paradise* indeed!' Pandit ji snorted, torn between expressing amusement at his wisecrack and disappointment on seeing the bungalow. Munshi's never-ending praise over the last two days had led him to expect something grander than what was before his eyes. What a pity!

Everything about it, like the elusive paradise, was incongruent. A single-storeyed, sprawling red bungalow was barely visible behind an overgrown garden. Undoubtedly it had been a beauty once, boasting of a high ceiling and an elegant parapet dotted with brown-coloured ventilators. Now these were obscured by swathes of thick, black cobwebs. A masonry platform with a breezy verandah running on all sides added a twist to an otherwise staid building. But grime-encased, metal grills caging it destroyed the sense of airiness. The crimson red paint had peeled off in parts in a pattern that made the exposed white patches look like pockmarks. It was, as if, the creator had designed a masterpiece and then set out to destroy its charm bit by bit.

Yet, if you look long enough, you will find a trace of beauty even in the ugliest object. So was the case with 'Paradise'.

Its redemption was a curved driveway leading to the porch that continued to the back of the house. It was a vision to behold—paved with red bricks and lined with a profusion of *parijaat* trees; their branches hung low, weighed down by the wispy, orange-white blossoms; whose exquisite beauty jarred with the gloom and decay of the setting. It was almost as if they were co-conspirators, trying to hide the hideousness of the building. And having failed to do so, they did the next best thing—created a diversion with a burst of colour and fragrance.

'Wait! Are you sure we are at the right place? Could there be a mistake in the address?' Pandit ji asked hopefully.

'No, Pandit ji… This is Dr Bimal Sen's bungalow. The one I told you about. I know it looks a *little* ramshackle. Ok, maybe more than a little, but nothing that a bit of plaster and a coat of paint will not cure.'

'Munshi,' Pandit ji was exasperated, 'I admit, I am an ardent admirer of your ability to make a situation look better than what it is. Believe you me, it's a useful quality in our profession. However, this is not the time to play games. I fear it will need much more than plaster and paint. After talking to you yesterday, I got the impression that it would be ready to move in with my family. I really don't know how…'

'Don't judge the house so hastily, Pandit ji. In the twenty years that we have worked together, have I ever let you down? Haven't *you* said on many an occasion that I have an uncanny eye for the best clients? I am telling you Pandit ji, this is a great bargain. Where else will you find a bungalow like this for the price they are demanding? Or the price we are willing to pay? I agree it is not as good as the Peeli Kothi we visited yesterday, but you have always said that appearances can be deceptive. For the price that we are offering, this is a far superior deal. Trust me!'

Pandit ji acquiesced all good sense that seemed to have prevailed in his life until then. Those who knew him were bemused. They asked, 'why?'

Why?

Why is the sky blue? Or the ocean so deep?

Sometimes the most complex, existential mysteries of the universe have the simplest explanations.

It could be that in the spring of 1975, the air was heady; fragrant with the delicate smell of *raat-ki-rani* and *parijat* flowers dangling from the trees that dotted Bangla Number Unnees. There was also numerology to provide answers to the unknown—the numbers 19 and 75 share a high affinity. It was possible that in a season marked by the end of the Vietnam War and the rise of the cruel Khmer Rouge on faraway shores, this weed-grown driveway of a derelict bungalow with its fragile parijat blossoms, was reminiscent of a sublime serenity. A symbol of all that mankind was willing to forfeit in pursuit of its ruthless ambition.

Or perhaps, Pandit Dinanath Awasthi was exhausted. Tired of a large, brabbling family in a small, rented house, he was convinced that it was time to create memories in a home of his own. A home that he could afford with his meager earnings as a fledgling advocate; no matter if it was cracked and crumbling.

Against his better judgment, succumbing to Munshi's advice yet again, Pandit ji appended his flourishing signature to a cheque and secured a place in 'Paradise'.

As they shifted into the rambling, eight-bedroom house, the family discovered how right *and* how wrong Munshi had been.

'It is entirely Munshi Shyamlal's fault. Ever since he has joined Pandit ji, he has brought all kinds of trouble. It is true that he is effective in the court. Pandit ji says that he can reel in wealthy clients like fish on a line. But this time, he has crossed all limits. How dare he call this hovel a bungalow?'

'It's okay, Mata ji.' Chhaya tried to pacify her mother-in-law. 'It's not as bad as we thought. First of all, Pandit ji finds it more convenient to reach the court from here. I've noticed that there is hardly any traffic on the main road. And then, the children's school is close by. They walk down in the morning without any difficulty. Most importantly, when Sumi, Vinu or Anu would come with their children, we are going to have all this space. The old house used to feel so cramped.'

Mata ji visibly brightened at the very mention of her beloved daughters.

'Hmm. That, at least, is something to celebrate. But I tell you, Munshi did this deliberately so that I shall have no peace for the next few years. All my hair will turn grey trying to bring this house in order.'

Despite Mata ji's qualms about the house, it took only a few weeks for the dilapidated, run-down Paradise to start glowing like a young bride. Neglect by its erstwhile owner had almost killed it. Pandit ji and his family seemed to have given it a new lease of life. Their love and care changed the weather-beaten bungalow into a vibrant home; gradually, the name 'Paradise', reminiscent of its ugly yesteryears, was forgotten and it came to be known as 'Pandit ji's Haveli'.

AN ASTROLOGER IN PARADISE

'*Suniye ji!* You must come home in time today. Are you listening to me?'

'Do I have a choice, dear? You are loud enough to be heard in Tiwari ji's house.'

'Haan, Haan! Let Tiwari ji also hear me. Let him know that my husband does not want to acknowledge anything that I have to say. And as for my "deafening" voice, you always complain that I shout. Unlike your darling sister and mother, I was never gagged in my father's house. Is it my fault that my father was the Zamindar of Bageechabad and he treated me like a son? I could say what I wanted to and however loudly I wished to,' Mata ji sniffed.

'You should have thought of this before you married me. My father never lied to you about me. He never said— "This girl will sit and embroider cushions—butter won't melt in her mouth." My father...'

The argument was veering towards a dangerous territory. Mata ji's sniffles were becoming louder and louder.

Without wasting any more time, Pandit ji interrupted, '*Nahi*, *Nahi*! Of course not. Your father was a gem, may his soul rest in peace! By the way, wasn't your brother supposed to visit this week?'

Pandit ji was acclaimed for his nimble wits. Many an adversary had been vanquished in the arena of the courtroom by this trait. At the moment, he was using all his skills to defuse a potentially explosive situation.

His effort was rewarded. Mata ji's face brightened up a bit. But she was not one to capitulate so soon or so easily.

'Hmm, in spite of your hectic schedule, you have managed to remember that Chhote Bhaiyya is coming today. Chalo, all is not lost. I wanted you to come home in time today precisely for this reason. I know you are one of the busiest lawyers of Aamnagri...'

As Pandit ji made to protest, Mata ji held up an imperious hand and swept on like the rampaging waters of the Kosi.

'I tell you, your flourishing legal practice is of no avail if you can't find time for your near and dear ones. Who will be by our side when we are on our deathbed? Definitely not your clients, though their pockets be stuffed with notes. Mark my words, it will be your kith and kin.'

'Aha! And here I thought that your new-found passion for social service was prompted by altruism! Didn't you attend a meeting of the Mahila Brahmin Sabha yesterday? And distributed old clothes and books at the Ladies Club last week? Hmm, this is the secret behind your appearances at charity programmes. Preparing for D-day in earnest, Mata ji? I must say, your foresight is commendable.'

Mata ji's flushed countenance and gaping mouth provided a perfect getaway. Taking advantage, Pandit ji beat a hasty retreat to the sanctuary of his office.

***

A wise man is one who knows when to attack and when to defend. Above all, he knows when to wave the white flag.

At 5 o' clock in the evening, Munshi found Pandit ji packing up.

'What happened, Pandit ji? Are you feeling all right? Are you going home early?'

'Yes, Munshi. I am perfectly fine. But I must leave.'

'You cannot, Pandit ji,' Munshi was alarmed. 'Ratan Lal is coming to finalise the arguments for his case. It is up for hearing tomorrow morning in the Family Court.'

'Tell Mr Ratan Lal that if I stay back to hear the details of his divorce case, then I will be preparing for the annulment of my own marriage. Chhote Bhaiyya is coming today from Bageechabad and I have been warned by *Her Ladyship* that if I am not home in time, my spirit will not find solace even after reaching the netherworld.'

'Oh! Of course,' Shyamlal's furrowed brow smoothened. 'You must leave at once then. I hear, Mata ji has arranged for an interesting surprise for Chhote Bhaiyya. Didn't you know? No, no, Pandit ji, you won't be hearing about it from me.'

Guffawing loudly, Munshi went back to sorting through the case papers in front of him.

It was an extremely puzzled Pandit ji who ran into his eldest daughter-in-law, Chhaya on his arrival at the Haveli.

'Pandit ji, you are back early. Should I get you some tea? I was just making a cup for Chhote Mama.'

'Has he come? Where is he?'

'Chhote Mama is with Mata ji in your room. Why don't you go ahead and join them? I'll get your tea inside.'

Loud laughter greeted Pandit ji as he moved towards his room. A stray thought flitted, light as a butterfly, across the landscape of his mind—though married for thirty-seven years, he had never been able to make his wife laugh like this. Perhaps the only time she felt truly at ease was in the company of her younger brother.

He owned this mansion where his four sons, their wives and progeny lived with him, his three daughters visited with their families, his four dogs frolicked around, where the kitchen was well-stocked and all the necessities of life were fulfilled. Yet, at that moment, Pandit ji felt a sickening vacuum within. He was besieged with regret.

Had he failed where it mattered the most?

'Isn't Pandit ji coming home?'

Shrugging aside his musings, Pandit ji took his cue, 'Here I am, Chhote Bhaiyya. How can I take the liberty of being late when you are a guest in my house?'

After the customary greetings and pleasantries had been exchanged over tea, Mata ji cleared her throat.

'I have a little surprise for you, Chhote Bhaiyya. During your last visit, you mentioned the new *Bhrigu Samhitā* office in Aamnagri. Remember? You wanted to go there but couldn't find time. Today, I've invited an astrologer who practices the art of reading horoscopes. He will tell you everything that you want to know from the past, present and future.'

'Horoscopes can be horror-scopes,' Pandit ji cackled. 'Do you really believe in this nonsense?'

Two pairs of identical eyes turned on him, one angry and accusatory, the other incredulous. Pandit ji hastily backtracked.

'I mean, I hope this person is a reliable fellow.' He added lamely, 'You know how these things can turn out to be.'

'He may not be as reliable as the witnesses you tutor for the court,' Mata ji was witheringly scornful. 'However, he can be trusted to speak the truth, something that you have, perhaps, forgotten after so many years of uttering…'

'Jijji! What are you saying?' Chhote Bhaiyya was aghast. He hastily tried to change the subject, 'Who is this learned sage? When is he arriving?'

As if on cue, Chhaya came in and announced, 'Mata ji, your guest has arrived. I have seated him in the drawing room.'

Pandit ji winced at the thought of an ash-smeared sadhu sitting on his cream, chintz-covered sofa. But he wisely held his tongue. Sighing deeply, he made a mental note to tell Munshi to buy some inexpensive runners for the sofas.

***

'Pranam, Baba. I'm so glad that you could find some time to visit us. I have heard so much about you from our neighbour, Mrs Tiwari. Please meet…'

'Baba knows everything. Who you are, who they are…' With his *Yoga Danda*, the holy man gestured towards Pandit ji and Chhote Bhaiyya.

'This world is nothing but a mirage in which we see ourselves. But what we see is not our true forms. It is a mere shadow, a reflection. Fools get taken in by the outer covering which is nothing but a hollow shell. Ah! These things cannot be learnt in one sitting.'

Impatiently, with an imperious wave, he motioned to Mata ji to sit at his feet on the floor. Mata ji hastily complied. Chhote Bhaiyya followed reluctantly.

'I'll send some water and fruit for Baba ji.' Pandit ji escaped into the adjacent room from where he could discreetly watch the entire proceedings. The thought of finding the meaning of life while gazing at the mud-stained feet of a necromancer was abhorrent to him and he refused to do so even for the sake of keeping marital peace.

'I will have to have a word with Tiwari tomorrow,' Pandit ji muttered to himself. 'The old chap needs to check his wife's philosophical leanings. Or at least ensure that they remain within the boundary of *his* house. I can't afford to have her put these absurd ideas into Mata ji's head. *Baba worship*!' He turned his attention back to the scene unfolding on the other side.

'Baba ji, we are indeed honoured to receive you at our humble abode.'

'You are a true believer, good woman. But you are tormented by a terrible weight on your mind.' Mata ji looked perplexed, while the Baba continued.

'Ever since you left your father's house thirty-five years ago, you have never felt at home.'

Mata ji's eyes turned moist.

'This is your brother. He does not live with you. You wish that he did, so that you could unburden yourself to someone; so that you could share your pain with a loved one. Your husband does not understand you.'

Pandit ji stared at the curtain, flabbergasted. He was at a loss for words. Though his lips were moving, no sound emerged. After a few moments, he regained control and turned towards Chhaya.

'The old coot! What he is saying would apply to all the women in this world!'

Chhaya giggled and went into the drawing room with a glass of water on an ornate silver tray that was used for only special guests.

The Baba was droning, 'You have four sons and four daughters. The women are not born of you. Your own daughters number three; they live in different cities to the south.'

'Now that's an intelligent guess, considering that there is only Nepal in the north. All other places have to be in the south,' Pandit ji muttered.

However, Mata ji had heard enough. Baba's omniscience about her family had put her mind at rest. She saw it all as clear as daylight. This man was truly gifted.

'O venerable one! You are aware of everything. I am indebted to you for coming here today. This is my brother, Ashok. But you already know that. Baba ji, he needs your blessings. He is beginning a new venture and we want to—'

Instead of uttering the customary blessing, the miracle-man started shivering.

'Arre! What happened Baba ji? Are you all right? Are you feeling cold?' Mata ji directed a baffled stare at Chhote Bhaiyya, begging for an explanation.

But he looked equally dumbfounded. It was unsettling to see a man shiver in the warmth of a balmy April evening.

Mata ji realised that it was futile to expect any assistance from her brother.

She called out to her bahu, 'Chhaya, O Chhaya! Run and get a blanket.'

The spasms had become more pronounced. The sadhu's body was jerking like a puppet on a string.

Suddenly, he shrieked, 'My child! You are in great peril. An evil spirit has cast its eye upon you. I see great danger. I see dark clouds, black smoke. A shadowy figure follows you.' His high-pitched voice ended in a crescendo— 'Beware! Yamaraj follows you.'

Mata ji and Chhote Bhaiyya were stunned. After an interminable silence, it was the hermit who spoke.

'Do not be alarmed. Baba has a cure for everything.'

He closed his eyes and started speaking in a flat, lifeless voice as if reading from an invisible script.

'I see blood. I see dust. A temple. You drove here by car. On the way, you passed a village. Your car rammed into a goat.'

'Uhh. Baba ji, did you really see this? I mean, I'm sure. Of course, you have supernatural powers. You must have seen everything. But wait! Please let me explain. It was like this. My driver is a careless man. A stupid, ignorant, careless fool. He was driving too fast. That goat jumped out of nowhere, right in front of the car. I know, I know, Didi. I guess I should have stopped. No, no actually, I'm sure I should have stopped. And given the animal's owner some compensation. The careless man! I mean the owner. Not looking after his goat, allowing it to run about on the road. No, no, I agree. He was an innocent, poor villager. It's my driver who is to blame. I assure you, I wanted to pay the owner money. But there was no one around. Uhh, no one. I swear I didn't see a soul! And no one was hurt,' Chhote Bhaiyya was shamefaced and sounded a trifle defensive.

'No one was hurt?' Baba ji thundered. 'How dare you say that? Do you realise that you killed a divine being? That goat was Goddess Lakshmi strolling on earth.'

'Really! Goddess Lakshmi! I think I made a big mistake. No, no, by looking at your face I can *see* that I made a big mistake. Goddess Lakshmi? On earth? I'm sorry, Baba ji. It looked like an ordinary goat. No, you are right. It was Goddess Lakshmi. At that time I did not realise it.'

'Oh, Baba ji!' Mata ji prostrated herself in front of the glowering ascetic. 'It's entirely my fault. I had told him to hurry. He was rushing here on my request. Is there some way we can atone for this terrible sin that he has unknowingly committed?'

Baba ji smiled. For Mata ji, the sun reappeared in a storm-darkened sky.

'You are a very intelligent woman, Mata ji. I could see that from the very first moment I laid my eyes upon you. There is a panacea for every ailment if the sadhu is powerful. But it will have a price. Are you ready to pay it?'

'Anything, Baba ji. Anything.'

By now, Pandit ji could see where this was heading. Clearly. Very, very clearly!

'The only way to atone for this horrific crime is to donate a goat made of solid gold to the Bhairon Temple in Phoolpur, on the night of the full moon.'

'What? A goat made of solid gold!' Chhote Bhaiyya exclaimed. 'Isn't there some other way, Baba ji? This is a little outside my budget.'

Baba fixed a beady eye on Chhote Bhaiyya.

'Do you wish to negotiate with Goddess Lakshmi?'

'Yes. I mean no.' Suddenly remembering his role, Chhote Bhaiyya supplicated himself before Baba ji.

'I've just started a new business of exporting mangoes, Baba ji. The first unit came up in Bageechabad last week. I need Ma Lakshmi's blessings. Yours too.' He hastily added.

'Yes. Your business is in danger. But more than that, your life is in danger. Vishnu is annoyed, very annoyed.'

'Vishnu? Why should my driver be annoyed? He is to blame for this trouble to begin with. The rascal should have been more careful.'

Chhaya looked at Pandit ji in alarm; he seemed to be in the throes of some kind of convulsions. He waved her away and pointed towards the gap in the curtain from where they had a ring-side view. The scene on the other side demanded unmitigated attention.

'You fool! I'm talking about Lord Vishnu, the Preserver of this Universe. You have killed his wife. He is on the verge of unleashing his fury upon you.'

'Baba ji, please help my brother,' Mata ji wailed. 'It is our good fortune that you have come here today. The gods have sent you. Please bestow your benediction upon us.'

'O kind woman, all these men are prospering only because you stand beside them as a pillar of strength. I have come here today drawn by your heartfelt invitation. Ordinarily, I would never intervene in a matter involving such a grave sin. Killing Goddess Lakshmi herself! Shiv, Shiv! You cannot begin to imagine how heinous his transgression is. Yet, I will have to help this wretch because of your good karma.

Listen carefully. I will have to perform a special ceremony to atone for his sins. I shall go to the temple of Bhairon and beg Him for forgiveness. At the same time, you must fast for the next five Fridays and Mondays and pray for your brother's safety.'

'But why should Bhairon get involved? Shouldn't we pray to Vishnu—'

Mata ji dug a fierce elbow into her brother's ribs. Trust these stupid men to say the wrong thing. No sense of timing. She quickly touched the saint's feet to divert his attention.

Baba had knitted his brows together when Chhote Bhaiyya started to speak. But Mata ji's gesture brought a smile to his lips.

'Oh Baba ji!' Tears of joy and relief flowed down Mata ji's face as she sensed that she was on the brink of victory. 'You have saved us from a great calamity. How can we ever thank you?'

'That is all right. Now I must be off. It is time for me to commence my evening prayer.'

'But Baba ji, you haven't eaten anything. Please share our humble meal tonight.'

'That husband of yours left to get me some fruit eons ago. He is nowhere to be seen. And you are asking me to stay for dinner!' Baba ji was sullen.

'Chhaya? Chhaya? Where is the fruit? The blanket? Oh yes! The blanket. Would you like me to wrap it around you, Baba ji? My husband remains a little distracted. Please do not hold it against him.'

Panic-stricken, Mata ji tried to assuage the ascetic. She cursed Pandit ji under her breath. They already had one sinner in Chhote Bhaiyya. Did he have to exacerbate the situation by disappearing so irresponsibly?

'Don't worry, I shall not put the evil eye on Pandit ji. These men are ignorant. They are safe because of you and your good deeds. Now if you will see off a learned man in the proper way— I'm getting late for my prayers.'

'Of course. Chhaya! Bring my purse.'

Pandit ji watched as his wife took out two crisp hundred-rupee notes and laid them at Baba's feet. He kicked the money aside with anger.

'Is this all your brother's life is worth? I shall leave you both to gift the golden goat yourself. Or perhaps, you prefer a wooden bier.'

That did the trick. With a cry, Mata ji emptied the contents of the purse at Baba's feet. Baba pocketed around six thousand rupees and stood up, swathed in the Merino wool blanket.

Before they could say 'Baba' again, he was gone. Truly an example of the *Invisible Force*!

With a wry smile, Pandit ji stepped out from behind the curtains.

'The surprise was a little expensive, wasn't it? And nasty, if I may say so! But what's a few thousand rupees to hear what one wants to?'

THE SARI WITH A TEMPLE BORDER

'Oooh! This is your prettiest sari, Mummy.'

'Thank you, Chikoo! When you grow up, you may wear it.'

'Really, Mummy? I love you so much. You are the best mummy in the world!'

'Thank you, my little princess. Flattery will get you everything.'

'Hee, hee! But I have never seen you wear it. It simply hangs in your cupboard. Why don't you wear it?'

'Now let me get ready or I shall be late for the wedding and Papa will be angry.'

Indu tried to gently remove herself from her daughter's affectionate embrace as Chikoo clung on determinedly.

'Only if you tell me why you never wear this sari even though it is one of the best that you have.'

'I'll tell you another time, Chikoo. Let me go now.'

'Do you have to go? Can't you stay till bed-time?'

'I wish I could, darling. But I must go. Do you want mummy to get a scolding for being late?'

'Of course not, Mummy! But I want you to stay with me for some more time. Please.'

The soft loving request would have melted the hardest of hearts. Indu hugged her daughter tightly. She thought for a minute and then used the oldest trick known to mothers.

'Let me tell you a story. Now that's my good girl. Why don't you sit on the bed and watch me get ready while I spin you a yarn?'

'Mummy, will you tell me the secret behind your sari? Please tell me its tale. Please?'

'If I do, will you go to sleep? I'll return from the wedding very quickly. You won't even realise I'm gone.'

'All right. I'll do whatever you tell me if you narrate the story.'

'Fine. Here it goes.

As you know, Pandit ji is very fond of playing bridge…'

***

'Chedilal, tell Sunder to wait with the car. I'll go to Dr Saxena's house around 7 o'clock to play bridge.'

'Ji, Pandit ji. Anything else?' Chedilal looked at Pandit ji with concern. He had never seen him so foul tempered.

'No,' Pandit ji was curt. 'Just shut the door behind you. I don't wish to be disturbed.'

Pandit ji stared at the closed door for a long time. Chedilal had worked for him for over a decade and meant well. He regretted his brusqueness with the old fellow and was tempted to call him back to apologise. But he was sapped and could barely muster the strength to stand. He placed a hand on the table for support.

He felt restless, as if his spirit wanted to break free from his body and run away far into the distance. At the same time he was exhausted. His legs felt numb, incapable of bearing his weight. Passing a weary hand over his eyes, he sank into his favourite leather armchair. But comfort eluded him. The chair's springy softness felt cold and alien today.

He looked out of the window of his study. A brick wall covered with a leafless creeper stared back. In the late afternoon, the sun was on the other side of the house leaving this area in semi-darkness. It matched his piqued mood, a gloomy shadow that followed him incessantly.

Like most people, he was susceptible to the occasional bouts of ennui. But this time it was different. It was a weight on his shoulders that no amount of laughter and sunshine seemed to dissipate. He tried to shrug it off. He immersed himself deeper into work. He gave up when the words in his clients' records began to dance in front of his eyes. He made another attempt by seeking company at home; only to discover that he no longer had the patience to handle young children. After a seemingly endless week spent snapping at those around him, the apathy persisted, unabated. Even the arrival of Saturday, his weekly bridge date, failed to cheer him up. Rather, the evening loomed ahead like a tiresome chore; one that he had to get through.

At Dr Saxena's soiree, Pandit ji sat quietly, letting the voices wash over him, without absorbing the words or their meaning. He hawed and hummed occasionally, pretending to be deeply engrossed in the game of bridge. In reality, he was thousands of miles away. Halfway through the evening, he secretly patted himself on the back. It was not an easy task to deflect attention from his burdened spirit. Then he caught his friends staring at him. His face flamed. Did he say something ridiculous?

He made a feeble attempt to inject some levity into the situation, 'Did I just sprout a moustache or something?'

The others continued to look fixedly at him.

Then his host spoke up. '*Kya hua,* Pandit ji? Did you lose an important case?'

When Pandit ji remained silent, Mr Singh pitched in good-naturedly, 'Or did Munshi fail to net a big, fat client today? Seriously Pandit ji, Munshi is a gem. It is said that with him around, your legal practice churns out more money than a note-printing machine. Then why the gloomy visage? *Dost, phir ye afsurdah surat kyun*? If a forced bachelor like me can smile and make merry, then you have so much to thank the Almighty for.'

Observing Pandit ji's raised eyebrows, Mr Singh added with a wink, 'A bubbling home filled with your progenies to carry the family name forward. A roaring practice with an unimpeachable reputation in Aamnagri especially in the Brahmin Sabha. When I look at you, I wonder why I am mirthful at all, for I have little in comparison, except the company of old friends and the Old Monk.'

Everyone in the vicinity burst out in high-decibel-laughter at this, prompted without doubt by the fine quality-Old Monk flowing freely.

'Singh Saab, life is not always as straightforward as it appears. You have peace of mind, which is a rare commodity. Do you realise that though I live in a joint family with four sons, I am the sole breadwinner? With the exception of Sudheer, who has joined the Indian Army, my sons are yet to settle in life. I'm a troubled man.'

'You agonise too much over a trifling matter, Pandit ji. Randheer, Sumeet and Vineet are fine boys, following in your footsteps. They will carry on your practice and hand over the baton to their next generation. I can see the sign that will hang outside your law office one day—M/S Awasthi, Awasthi & Awasthi—three generations of legal practitioners in Aamnagri!'

'Saxena, at least *you* spare me these pipe dreams. I know better than anyone else that one does not become a successful lawyer merely by studying law and wearing a black coat. Even today, I can recall every obstacle that I've stumbled against to reach this point in my career. I have laboured for decades to earn this rest. These boys think it is child's play. They aren't willing to struggle. They don't realise that once I am gone, no one will spare them a second glance.'

'Hmm, I see that may be a genuine problem. What about *Bhabhi* ji? Can't she talk some sense into them?'

Pandit ji sighed. He had no response to his friend's questions.

Little did he know that a discussion raging in the adjacent room was throwing up all the answers! For women are celestial beings, conferred with divine powers of discernment. Had Pandit ji paid attention to the confabulation happening a mere six feet away, he would have been an enlightened man. Alas! He had not the privilege to hear Mrs Rama Saxena and her younger sister, Lily, schmoozing in the dining room.

'I tell you Lily, Mrs Awasthi is the worst kind of snob. She thinks it is below her stature to associate with us. That is the real reason for her not joining us for these Saturday-night dinners.'

'I'm not sure, Didda. Pandit ji is such a good man. He has known Jija ji since they were boys. How can he permit his wife to dictate to him?'

'That's exactly what I tell Mr Saxena. Pandit ji is a thorough gentleman. His wife, Shakuntala, however is a different kettle of fish. She chooses to be called "Mata ji of the Haveli". Truth be told, there is not a maternal bone in her body. The way she treats her children, she would put Hitler to shame.

A niece of Mr Saxena's sister, who lives in Bageechabad, told me that Mrs Awasthi is a famous name there. She hails from an aristocratic family known for their wealth and powerful connections. During the British rule, they ruled over more than a thousand villages and controlled most of the mango orchards. Her father, who is now dead, God bless his soul, was called the "Zamindar" of Bageechabad. She was his first-born so despite his wife's warnings, he pampered her to no end. She grew into a free-spirited livewire, a la *Hunterwali.* Seated on her favourite horse, Shakuntala rode through the length and breadth of her father's Zamindari as a young girl. Unfortunate villagers who dared to cross her path were soundly whipped with her *chabuk.* While marriage has taken her away from horses, it has done little to rein in her temper. Many a servant working in the Haveli has had a taste of her chabuk-like tongue. That is the reason no helper stays with her for more than a few months.'

'Really! Is this true?'

'Of course. Why would I lie, Lily? And this applies not just to the servants but also to the other members of her family.'

'But they have a large household. Surely, *someone* must have the courage to stand up to her.'

'For a long time, I thought so too. I've known the family for more than twenty years. Now I realise that each member of Pandit ji's Haveli deals with Shakuntala differently.

Pandit ji has struck a deal with the devil herself. He leaves Shakuntala alone as long as she does not disturb him. In exchange, she settles all wrangling matches with the servants outside his hearing.

Then, there are the four sons. As children, they were petrified of her. Once they stepped out into the world, they discovered that their mother was no more than a bully. The other day, I overheard Vineet likening her to a pesky tenant, who tries to occupy as much space as she can. These irreverent boys have dealt with Shakuntala's fits of fury just as one would unceremoniously evict an unwanted paying guest.'

Lily giggled. The image of Mrs Awasthi being booted out was too incongruous even for her fertile imagination.

'Is it true that she is mortally scared of Pandit ji? I've heard that the mere threat of reporting something to him is enough to send her packing to her brother's house for at least two weeks.'

They both tittered and went back to laying the dinner table in companionable silence. It was short-lived because neither could suppress her curiosity for long.

'You have not said much about her *bahus*, Didda,' Lily observed.

'I thought you knew them better than me,' Rama gave a condescending smile.

'Aha! Have you also heard…'

Rama's conspiratorial glance was all the encouragement that Lily needed.

'I've known their eldest bahu, Chhaya, for the last eighteen years. Our association goes back to the time she first came to the Haveli after marriage. She is a cool customer, Didda. Her mother was a schoolteacher and she came well tutored. In those days, I used to call her *teekhi mirchi*. You can laugh all you like, Didda, but she has used a singular mix of sugar, spice and chillies to handle the family.

In the presence of Pandit ji, she was sugar—the demure and docile bahu, who observed all the norms of filial duty. Her spicy relationship with her husband, Sumeet, Pandit ji's second son, ensured that he stood by her, much like the Rock of Gibraltar, in all her disputes with Mata ji.

And when the need arose, her sharpness in rebuking Mata ji was nothing short of red-hot chili paste on the palate.'

As Lily paused for breath, Rama twittered self-righteously, 'There is karma in this world.'

'Indeed, Didda. One would have thought that God would have been kind to Mrs Awasthi the next time around. But no, her second bahu, Varsha, is no better. She got married to Randheer, the eldest son, about twelve years ago.'

'Of course! It was a grand wedding. At the time, you were too young to hear the scurrilous tales that were spread. It was…'

'Didda,' Lily wryly interrupted, 'I was young, not deaf and blind! The whole world knew that Randheer was keen on marrying that Punjabi girl.'

Mrs Saxena gasped audibly. 'So the rumours were true! People said that she was a real beauty. How in the world did he agree to marry Varsha then?'

Lily warmed up to her story and continued, 'Mrs Awasthi declared that his marriage to Harleen would happen over her *dead body*. Very much like Bollywood! After a lot of theatrics, Randheer caved in. Enters Varsha.

Ordinarily, Varsha's charms would have driven out all thoughts of that Punjabi *kudi* from his mind. It's a pity, Randheer stuck to the Bollywood script of *Devdas* instead of *Silsila*. He shunned Varsha and immersed himself in liquor and work, in that order.

In the beginning, Varsha was indulgent. But she is not a moron. She soon figured out that her husband's devotion to work stemmed from a broken heart. At last, after a few probing questions, the truth came out!

You know, Didda, the day Varsha heard about Harleen, she was livid. She accused Pandit ji of deliberately destroying her life. From that day, Varsha became Pandit ji's *Shikhandi*, his nemesis. His guilt does not allow him to look her in the eyes. Tormented by his conscience, Pandit ji forbade Mata ji from uttering a single word of reproach in Varsha's presence. Mata ji dared not disobey Pandit ji. After all, she was responsible for his predicament.

Varsha, on the other hand, decided to make the best of a bad situation. Armed with this knowledge, she took full advantage of Mata ji's helplessness and did as she pleased.'

The clink of china did not interfere with the sisterly exchange.

'I've heard that the third girl is much better, though. After these two bahus, perhaps, the Lord thought that a chastened Shakuntala deserved some respite.'

'Truer words were never spoken, Didda. Except that a leopard can't change its spots, and neither can Mata ji change her nature. Indu is a gem of a person; her radiant looks a perfect foil to her inner beauty. But sadly, due to these very qualities she was doomed. She attracted the hostility of the Haveli's female bastion from the day she arrived.

Unlike Chhaya, she was neither sugar nor chilies. Her husband's presence in the Haveli did not shield her either. Sudheer's job in the Army kept him away for prolonged periods.

All in all, she was the perfect target for Mata ji.'

'It's a small world. I knew Indu as a young girl,' said Rama. 'Our families were neighbours in Chandoli. Very decent and well-mannered people! Due to her sheltered upbringing, she is not very street-smart. She is quite forthright and lacks the arsenal of sugarcoated quinine tablets in her vocabulary, unlike her sisters-in-law. There isn't an ounce of meanness in her body. As a result, she can't imagine being rude to her husband's mother. Not even when she receives an out-and-out tongue lashing many times a day.'

Lily eagerly chipped in, 'Poor girl! It is true that her gifts have proved to be her undoing. Apparently, once Mata ji discovered that Indu cooks mouth-watering food, far better than anything she'd ever tasted, she sent the cook away. Her orders were that only Indu would cook for the dozen occupants of the Haveli and the four dogs thenceforth.'

'Ask Shakuntala if she can make even a cup of tea! Hmmph! I feel terrible for Indu,' said Rama.

'Yes, Didda! Life is not fair. As if this slavish drudgery was not enough, Indu's status has worsened ever since the youngest bahu, Madhu arrived. Did you know that my sister-in-law, Suchi, studied with her in college? The other day, Suchi and I had gone to buy some jewellery and met Madhu in the market. Suchi commented that the young lady is way ahead of her times. She has introduced…what were the words? Yes, "*outsourcing* and *delegation*" to Pandit ji's Haveli.

The onerous task of tackling Mata ji has been entrusted to Madhu's husband, Vineet, the youngest scion of Pandit ji's family, while Madhu is free to flit about irresponsibly, like a butterfly.'

'As I said, Lily, Shakuntala's is a classic case of just desserts. That haughty woman has never behaved decorously with people and today she is reaping what she sowed.'

'Do you think Pandit ji is privy to the occurrences in his house? Right under his nose?'

'I have serious doubts. Men are obtuse in such matters. You know, none of these ladies—Chhaya, Varsha or Madhu— are of an evil temperament. But like begets like. Have you seen children in a group who can't resist throwing stones at a lame stray dog? Similarly, when the three of them are together, they find the temptation of teasing and bullying Indu irresistible.

My cook has informed me that nowadays Indu is relegated to the kitchen making endless cups of tea and pakoras for her sisters-in-law and Shakuntala. To top it all, she is generously rewarded with barbs and insults.'

Tsk-tsking at the state of affairs and having completed a most satisfying session of psychoanalysis that would have made Freud proud, Mrs Saxena and Mrs Verma went back to the mundane task of feeding the hungry men.

Meanwhile, the menfolk continued to struggle with banal issues in the drawing room outside.

'Do you intend to go somewhere during the summer vacation, Pandit ji?'

'I've never visited South India. I thought this year I'd go to Madurai and Rameshwaram and perhaps, a couple of other places. Would any of you like to join me?'

***

Rule One: Absence makes the heart grow fonder.

Rule Two: The fondness is directly proportional to the duration of the absence.

Rule Three: The more enjoyment experienced during the absence, the greater the fondness on return.

After a self-indulgent, six-week vacation spent exploring the Indian peninsula, Pandit ji returned, feeling considerably more affectionate towards his family members, especially Mata ji. His return was hailed with a rousing reception—chanting of prayers, breaking of a coconut and the auspicious *arti*. After all, it was a homecoming following six long weeks of absence.

Unfortunately, the prolonged cacophony of the cymbals gave him a headache; when the coconut was smashed, it almost fractured his toe and certainly splattered his new silk *achkan,* and the smoke from the *arti* made him dizzy. Six weeks suddenly seemed abysmally short.

By the time Mata ji finished, Pandit ji was missing his solitary wanderings. He hastened to his room and collapsed like a ship without any wind in its sail. As he lay on the bed, he cursed that hour of madness when he felt the absence of his family, when the faithful husband and loving father had surfaced. He had thought to himself, what gift do I take for these wonderful women? For these docile beings that make my home a paradise. However, closer up, reality was harsh. During the arti today, they all looked more like Chandi than Menaka.

Uff! Pandit ji rued his temporary insanity. He had spent hours rummaging for the perfect gift. And then expended several thick wads of notes on acquiring it. At the time, it appeared flawless. Six yards of that handwoven magical garment—the sari! Presently, the seven cottons and one silk packed in his battered leather suitcase seemed a colossal waste of time, effort and money.

Here, a peek into Pandit ji's mind is imperative.

He was a man obssessed with method and symmetry. For him, things had to move in a preordained manner. A visitor to his office observed neatly stacked towers of case files created for each client, arranged alphabetically. Much like those meticulously paginated and neatly documented records, Pandit ji carried an office in his mind where the gifts were earmarked. The five cotton saris carried an invisible label each of Mata ji and the four bahus.

It should have ended at that. However, Pandit ji was a sucker for favourable deals. The discount on offer was impressive, so he allowed himself to be persuaded by the shopkeeper and bought two more cotton saris. They went into the mental drawers marked with the names of his widowed bhabhis.

In the end, just as he was leaving the shop, he was overwhelmed by an inexplicable burst of affection for Mata ji. That rascal of a shopkeeper seized the opportunity and sold him an expensive silk sari with the trademark Kancheepuram temple border.

Oh why?

He could have kicked himself. If only…

'I swear, I'll never accompany Saxena on a shopping jaunt. The fool! In his company, I too acted like a dunce. Why should three old men visit a sari shop is beyond me! Had that idiot not bought those saris for his wife and sister-in-law, I would have escaped.'

As Pandit ji lay lamenting his temporary dementia, Mata ji sauntered into the room. Her demeanour was akin to a Chinese queen whose prized Shih Tzu has been restored to her.

'Everyone is delighted to have you back, Pandit ji. This time your vacation felt longer than before.'

'Hmm. Long?'

'Very long,' she was firm. 'One realises the importance of one's loved ones when one is separated from them, isn't it?'

'Is it? Can love kill? Can one feel smothered by too much affection?'

'Did you say something?'

'No, no. Nothing! Ignore me. I am just tired.'

'You talk such nonsense after these trips. It's all that Singh and Saxena's doing. Stuffing your head with silly ideas! Do you realise what you said?' Mata ji laughed full-throatedly. 'How can the love of your sons and daughters kill you? You speak gibberish sometimes. Makes me wonder how you are the most famous lawyer of Aamnagri! Don't worry, Pandit ji. Take a nap. You will feel fine by tomorrow.'

'That's a good idea. But what are you doing?' Pandit ji cried out in alarm.

He was firmly pushed aside by a hard object.

Mata ji had dumped the contents of his suitcase on the bed where a minute earlier she was urging him to rest.

'Nothing. I am looking for my gift. Where have you concealed it?'

'Here, let me take it out.' Pandit ji was weary and resigned. 'It is best that we give Veena and Rita bhabhi their gifts now. The sooner they get them, the faster will they depart.'

In the ensuing moment of icy silence, Pandit ji knew he had committed the ultimate sin; he had suggested the unthinkable.

'Did you mention giving something to Veena bhabhi and Rita bhabhi?' In situations such as these, Mata ji drew upon the authority of all her dead ancestors whose sway once extended over a hundred villages. 'Have you forgotten?'

Pandit ji would have been proud of the cross-examination that followed, had *he* been the one conducting it. With impressive orderliness, Mata ji listed out all the wrongs that her two *jethanis* had inflicted upon her. She flatly refused to give them any presents. If Pandit ji insisted, he could do so over her *dead body*.

Pandit ji waspishly wished his wife would make her threat good this time. Then he recalled his deal with the devil and decided to buy peace.

Was she willing for an out-of-court settlement?

No.

Mata ji was as firm as Mount Kailash. After several moves and counter-moves, Pandit ji, the leading luminary of Aamnagri Bar, conceded the case.

Though not as gracious in defeat, Mata ji was magnanimous in victory. In a fit of generosity coupled with the necessity to reiterate her selfless credentials, she declared that *she* would not take any sari.

'I am growing old. So are your two bhabhis. Their motto should be simple living and pure thinking. Ostentation is best left to the youngsters. You should give the bahus one sari apiece. And when my dear Sumi, Vinu and Anu come, they can have the rest.'

A vanquished Pandit ji collapsed on the bed a second time, utterly trounced in battle.

***

'Hey, Chedilal! What has Pandit ji brought this time?'

'How would I know, Badi Bhabhi?' Chedilal knew when information had a price.

'You always know these things. Here, I've got you a cup of tea. Drink it quickly and tell me all that you know. You brought the bags inside.'

Chhaya could have wrung Chedilal's neck as he sipped his tea slowly, carefully relishing it. One day she would get her hands on…

'Indu bhabhi makes the best tea.'

'Yes, yes. I am aware of that. Now tell me quickly.'

Jealousy!

'Well, I couldn't see much, you know, as the suitcase was packed, but…'

'Yes? Hurry up, will you?'

Impatience!

'Pandit ji was carrying a plastic bag bearing the name of a sari shop.'

'Do you remember the label?'

Excitement!

'Can I get another cup of tea? No? Okay, okay. I think it was some Kancheepuram Sari Emporium. Where are you rushing off, Badi Bhabhi? You promised me another cup of tea.'

Wildfire was slower to spread than the news of Pandit ji's gifts. After all, it was an annual exercise and by now there was a well-established pattern for information dissemination: Chedilal to Chhhaya to Varsha and Madhu.

'Quick! There is no time to be lost. Speed is of essence,' Chhaya rushed to inform her two accomplices. 'In a day or two, Sumi, Vinu and Anu are expected to be here. Mata ji has asked them to come and meet their father. If we delay, you can be assured of getting the worst from the lot.'

'What should we do?'

'I'll tackle Mata ji. She loves to brag about Pandit ji's visit to Mrs Tiwari next door. Suggesting a neighbourly visit post lunch should be easy. You make sure Indu is out of the way.'

'How?'

'Use your imagination. *Arrey*, tell her to prepare Pandit ji's favourite *kaddu ki sabzi*. That should keep her occupied.'

***

Sleep can be magical. As the body rests, the mind wanders off to realms of beauty and tranquility. The sense of calmness persists after awakening. Rejuvenated after his siesta, Pandit ji regained some of his cheery disposition and tender feelings towards his progeny.

'Chedilal! Chedilal! Oh, there you are. Where are the bahus? Tell them that I want to see them.'

The entire episode was over in a few minutes.

Anticipating Pandit ji's summons, Chhaya, Varsha and Madhu lay siege in the nearby living room. At the first call, they rushed to his room. Mata ji was conveniently missing, having gone over for a visit to Mrs Tiwari's place. Indu's absence was suitably explained and magnanimously excused.

Those present were ordered to choose a sari of their liking. Not wanting to get further embroiled in a saga that should never have begun, Pandit ji busied himself with storing his ties and waited for the three ladies to finish. Chhaya, Varsha and Madhu eagerly picked up a sari. When they observed that four pieces were left, they looked at each other. Should we?

Madhu had several foibles but ambivalence was not one of them. She picked up another sari. Not to be outdone, the others did the same. Masking their glee beneath somber visages, their arms filled with the rustling cottons and their heads bowed, the three ladies quietly left the room.

Once out of earshot, Madhu sniggered. Chhaya and Varsha joined in and soon they were clutching their sides in irrepressible laughter.

'Indu will get a dreadful shock. As usual, she will receive the leftovers.'

'Only this time *there are no* leftovers! We've cleaned the whole plate.'

'Yes. The last piece was so drab. I wouldn't touch it even if someone put a gun to my head.'

As the trio returned to the living room, they bumped into Indu. She was rushing towards Pandit ji's room.

'Didi, did Pandit ji call me? Did he send for you? I was making his favourite kaddu ki sabzi, so I got late. Have you met him? I hope he's not angry that I did not come immediately.'

'Don't worry, Indu. You are dot on time. As always!'

'We explained to him that you were busy in the kitchen. It's good that you are always occupied. Wishing you many more such busy afternoons, my dear.'

Their tinkling laughter bore into her ears like a drill. The twin saris in their grip told a different tale. Indu realised that she had been deceived. Yet again.

'Where were you, Indu bhabhi? Why did you delay? Those vultures have picked the best parts,' Chedilal was morose.

Without a word, Indu knocked on the half-open door leading to Pandit ji's room. Misery battled with half-dead optimism.

'Come in.'

Indu entered and stood at the threshold with her head bowed. Pandit ji was still settling his ties, arranging them by colour, from light to dark. It was an old trick that calmed him down.

He gestured towards the table absent-mindedly, 'Pick one of your choice.'

The solitary cotton sari lying there looked forlorn. Abandoned.

Under other circumstances she might have liked it. It was

her favourite shade of green. But at that moment, it seemed to ridicule her status in the Haveli. Like that last piece, Indu felt discarded. Anger warred with decorum; self-righteousness with filial duty. Duty emerged victorious. Exercising great self-control, blinded with tears, she picked up the sari and began to walk out.

Yet, self-respect refused to concede defeat.

Suddenly, Indu felt an energy rise within her.

'What happened in that instant was inexplicable, Chikoo. It was, as if, I stood at a crossroads. I could choose to be the doormat, which others were determined to make of me. Or I could reclaim my rightful position as the mistress of the Haveli. I caught a glimpse of myself in the mirror in Pandit ji's room. I saw the invisible reflection of my children beside me—you and your brother. And then I did something that I had never thought possible in my wildest dreams. For the first time in my married life, I walked up to Pandit ji, touched his feet and looked him squarely in the eye ...'

'*Hum kyun*? Why me?'

Pandit ji was thrown off balance by this strange query. He was used to fielding Mata ji's googlies but he had never really paid much attention to this quiet mouse in his house. This question was out of syllabus.

'You are a fair man, Pandit ji. You preach and practice the principles of justice every day. You fight against wrong doing, so today, I demand justice in your Court. Each of your daughters-in-law has chosen two saris. Why am I left with one?'

Pandit ji was nonplussed. He looked at the vacant table. It had never occurred to him that his bahus would make a clean sweep and queer the pitch so thoroughly. But this girl in front of him had a valid argument. In the interest of fair play, she should get two saris.

Silence weighed heavily in that room for the second time that day.

Crossing over to his suitcase, Pandit ji took out the sari with the temple border, the one that he had lovingly purchased for his wife. He sighed deeply. It was true that the sari had cost him a fortune. But justice had to be meted out, no matter what the price. And Mata ji had already abnegated her claim. This was the way it ought to be.

'This is how I acquired this life-altering possession, Chikoo—the sari with the temple border.

Ever since, whenever Mata ji became too obnoxious, I would quietly remind her that Pandit ji would not appreciate such rude behaviour. As no one ever knew the full episode of how I had extracted the sari with the temple border from Pandit ji, they were all scared. At my tiniest reference to that incident, Mata ji would stop badgering me.

When I look back, I am struck by the implications of the incident. It brought an array of colours into my life. It made Mata ji see red, and my sisters turn green with envy. In many ways, this mustard and maroon sari was like a *tabeez*. It gave me the strength to stand up to their bullying. I realised that being well-mannered does not translate into sacrificing one's dignity.'

'Oh Mummy! Now it makes sense. I always wondered why you never wore such an exquisite sari. It hung in your cupboard all the time. We moved to different cities and different houses. Everything in our house changed, only the position of your sari remained unaltered. This is a marvelous account for a gorgeous sari.'

'I agree, Chikoo. Since that day, it is my strongest talisman. The sari with the temple border didn't change anything, but it gave me the courage to change *everything*.'

A GHOST IS FOND OF EGGS

Summers are special in Pandit ji's Haveli.

It is because much like the *Aamnagri chaat*, where individual ingredients are mixed to create a unique flavour, several reasons come together to make summers here out of the ordinary.

Beyond doubt, it is an extraordinary time of the year. The magnificent parijat trees scatter their fragile blossoms on the driveway, a silk carpet woven with orange and white threads alluring royal visitors. The branches of the mango trees are laden with green, half-ripe fruits that beckon to the children of the household. The setting sun casts its golden glow on the crimson-hued bungalow, and clear, pale skies gaze fondly upon its denizens.

Into this sylvan setting, every summer, Pandit ji's three daughters step in with their children in tow. They bring with them gift-laden suitcases and gossip from the cities. Their landing marks a relaxation in the otherwise strict daily routine of the Haveli. Everyone wakes up leisurely. With the High Court and school closed, there is no rush. The days begin with languorous conversations over tea and end with card games that continue late into the night. It is a time of grand celebrations and homecoming, when laughter and whispered conspiracies mingle with the sweet fragrance of the raat-ki-rani—a perfect backdrop for the bonhomie that pervades the Haveli as it plays host to Pandit ji's capacious clan.

This year, when salubrious summer tiptoed into Pandit ji's Haveli, it stopped in its tracks. Almost as if a signboard barring its entry was affixed heralding that this summer was going to be unlike any other. It watched cautiously from the sidelines.

Mata ji was in an unusually dour mood.

'Men will never learn. How many times have I told him not to spoil the summer *chhutti*?'

'*Kya hua, Mata ji*, what happened?' Chhaya had rarely seen Mata ji so despondent early in the morning.

'*Kya nahi hua, bahu*? What hasn't happened? Pandit ji has gone ahead and invited Rameshwar Babu and his family to come and stay with us this summer. Now where will we put up so many people? Sumi, Vinu and Anu are waiting for the children's school break to come here. I ask you, how can you have guests in the house at a time like this?'

'Isn't he one of Pandit ji's closest friends? The one who relocated to the United States after the death of his wife?'

Mata ji sat down forlornly. 'Yes. Rameshwar Babu's house was next to ours when we lived in Civil Lines. Relations between the two families go back two generations. Their grandfathers were bosom friends. Even after Rameshwar Babu settled in America, Pandit ji maintained close contact with him. So much so that when he was leaving, he entrusted the responsibility of his house to Pandit ji. After fifteen years, he is returning to Aamnagri this summer for a short break.'

Chhaya interrupted, 'His son is working in the US as an Engineer, isn't he?'

Mata ji nodded and carried on. 'Knowing that his house

would not be habitable, Pandit ji asked him to stay with us till everything was ready. I want to know, haven't we always kept the summers exclusively for the family? This is the only time when I can have my daughters and grandchildren with me. But Pandit ji has to play spoilsport,' Mata ji cried in a thin peevish voice.

Chhaya nodded sympathetically. She knew how much Mata ji looked forward to the summer vacations. As if all the love and affection that she kept bottled within her came pouring forth for her daughters and their brood during this brief period. Her stern veneer would slip away to disclose a cheerful and ebullient persona.

'You have a point, Mata ji. Having guests at this juncture would unnecessarily complicate things. Isn't there something we can do?'

'Nothing, my daughter. I may curse and grumble, but in my heart, I know that I cannot turn away Rameshwar Babu's family, especially when his deceased wife was such a dear friend of mine. Pandit ji also knows this, which is why he has played this trick.'

'Mata ji! Mata ji!' Gauri was using all her lungpower to summon the matriarch. 'Madhu bhabhi has slipped and fallen in the courtyard. I think she has broken her leg.'

With panic writ large on her face, Mata ji rushed out.

Today was definitely not a good day.

'God, give me the strength to accept things that I cannot change,' Chhaya uttered philosophically and set about making preparations for hosting not three, but four families that summer.

By evening, the Haveli was humming like a well-oiled machine. Mata ji was not the mistress of the Haveli without reason. Minor setbacks such as Madhu's confining to her room with a fractured foot did not deter her one whit. With military precision that would have delighted the German army, she got the rooms re-arranged. Separate dormitories were fashioned for the children, the women and the men. She even left an independent room for Rameshwar Babu and Pandit ji to play cards. After all, what kind of a reunion would it be without the mandatory bridge party?

Despite putting on a brave face for the world, Mata ji was conscious that with fifteen regular inhabitants, another twenty guests and three dogs, she had her hands full. She marshaled her troops and divided the responsibilities in the house.

'Chhaya, you will ensure that the arrangements for sleeping are taken care of. If it becomes unbearably hot in the evenings, some charpoys are to be put out in the courtyard under the shade of the old mango tree for the men and older children to sleep in. All bedding must be cleaned and ironed by the *dhobi*. I can't have bed-bugs crawling over the guests.

Varsha, you are responsible for the grocery and refreshments for the guests. Ask Chedilal to get a few packets of Parle-G biscuits and keep them in stock. Other snacks will be prepared in the house by Maharani. Make sure that supplies don't run out.'

Mata ji had saved the most difficult task for Indu— 'As for you Indu, since you are not capable of doing much, you will assist me in supervising the kitchen. Meals are to be prepared for all the guests and family members, snacks are to be served with tea and special care needs to be taken of our *videshi* guests.

Madhu, I know you have been told to rest and recuperate. I expect you to organise board games for the youngsters during the day. We cannot let them roam outside in this scorching sun. Or else, Vinu's mother-in-law will accuse me of turning her precious grandchildren into burnt toasts!

Chedilal, inform everyone that the staff is to report to work half an hour earlier than usual. No excuses will be accepted.'

Without waiting for a response, Mata ji stormed out of the room. Her army knew better than to argue and fell uneasily into formation.

***

Guests started trickling on the day schools closed. The first group reached from Rampur, where Pandit ji's youngest daughter, Anu had set up her house. She came with her four children and their pet dog, Lucy. The dog received a welcome as joyous as the children themselves. After all, it was a progeny of Pandit ji's prized German shepherd, Ruby. For almost a decade, Anu and Ruby triumphed in every dog show at Aamnagri. They were inseparable. So when Anu got married, naturally, her dowry included Ruby's pup, Lucy. It was unclear who was happier when Anu came to the Haveli—Mata ji, Ruby or Lucy? Amidst a noisy and happy assembly of both humans and canines, the summer festivities began.

Over the next few days, the two other daughters, Sumi and Vinu, descended with their brood and added to the merry chaos.

The Haveli strained at the seams. Residents were talking, arguing or relaxing in various rooms. Half-opened suitcases spilled their contents in hallways. People exchanged gifts, shared gossip and unburdened their souls. Adults remained indoors to escape the heat while the dogs and children frolicked in the lawns. None heeded Mata ji's dire pronouncements of darkened skin and the uncertain, ugly future of a spinster. This was Aamnagri where none wanted a dark bride! 'Fair' and 'convent-educated' were the minimum qualifications. But Mata ji's warnings went in vain as the atmosphere reverberated with carefree cries and laughter.

Despite all the hiccups, Mata ji was delighted. To have one's young ones and their offspring in the same house was a benediction of The Lord. She went around making sure that everything was perfect. She took extra care that siblings spent time with each other, while she and her efficient team looked after their worldly needs. It was a true holiday for her daughters, as they were freed from all responsibility and the burden of running a household. They relished every minute of it.

It was in this joyful chaos that Rameshwar Babu showed up with his son, daughter-in-law and their young grandson.

'It is a pleasure to have you back with us, Ramu,' Pandit ji was uncharacteristically verbose on meeting his childhood friend.

'You can't imagine how glad I am to be here, Pandit. The people, the city, the air we breathe in are like my kindred. The atmosphere seeps into my soul, and I feel the tug deep inside. I can't explain it but it is as if every blade of grass I've played on, or every drop of rain I've felt on my face calls out to me to return,' Rameshwar Babu paused as he tried to gain control over his emotions. He cleared his throat and continued, 'It is so kind of you to put us up in your house. I don't know what we would have done otherwise, with my own house in shambles. Do you remember Rohit and Seema? Seek Pandit's blessings, you two. And this is Kunal, on his maiden visit to Aamnagri.'

As the two men exchanged notes, Chhaya and Varsha were having a whispered chitchat in a corner.

'The daughter-in-law is nothing special. Quite nondescript if you ask me.'

'She might be living in the United States but her clothes are so ordinary.'

'Unfortunately, in this case, clothes do not make the man or the woman, my dear. Mata ji has issued strict instructions; they are to be treated like royalty. New mosquito nets, extra-white bedsheets and expensive bathing soaps have been purchased for them.'

'Yes. I've also heard that for fear of contracting a stomach infection, Mata ji has ordered that they should be given only boiled water to drink. Rameshwar Babu tried to refuse but you know how stubborn she can be.'

'I wonder how big their house in the States is. Do they have servants to help?'

'Hold your horses, Badi Bhabhi. They are here for five more days. We will have all the time in the world to ask them.'

As presaged by Mata ji, the arrival of Rameshwar Babu and his family inadvertently threw cold water on the activities of the adults. While the elderly and children mingled uninhibitedly, it was the young men and women who found it difficult to break the ice. Conversations were stilted; curiosity, tinged with envy, led to restrained and formal talks. The little ones and the dogs, however, continued to enjoy their vacations with the same unabated fervour.

***

The visit would have passed uneventfully and Rameshwar Babu would have gone to his own house after a week's stay at Pandit ji's Haveli. But what is the sultry summer without the tangy tamarind? So, the guests in Pandit ji's Haveli always associated that summer with the episode of the ghost who liked eggs.

Now it so happened that Rameshwar Babu's grandson, Kunal, lovingly referred to as Kony, had acquired a fondness for eggs. It was rather inexplicable in a family of vegetarians. His parents were unsure whether it was genetic—his maternal great-grandmother had been a meat-devouring Nordic—or if it was environmentally induced by his birth and upbringing in the carnivorous atmosphere of America. Perhaps, their Assamese neighbour complimented his oval, egg-shaped face, comparing it to a 'kony' or egg.

Though difficult to attribute the cause, the effect was the same—given a choice, Kony would feast on egg omelettes for breakfast, poached eggs for lunch and any form of eggs for dinner.

Unfortunately, in Pandit ji's Haveli, any form of non-vegetarian food was contraband.

After several days of forced vegetarianism, Kony's seven-year-old mind rebelled. He *wanted* eggs and he *must* have eggs. Period.

Kony's father, Rohit had adequately briefed Seema about Mata ji's iron-fisted governance. She was aware of her stern adherence to rituals and insistence on maintaining purity in the kitchen. Though she had been away from the land of '*atithi devo bhava*' for more than a decade, she knew all too well the true feelings of a hostess. The guest is equivalent to God only for the first few days. They had, in any case, overstayed. The repairs in their house were taking longer than expected. Now the Prasads were on thin ice in Pandit ji's Haveli. Realising this, she tried to divert her son.

It is said that children are like clay; they can be moulded into any form. Kony definitely subscribed to this truism. With a minor difference—*his* mind was to be shaped the way *he* wanted it and definitely not what his mother might be aiming at. The American love for liberty and independence had given him a will of his own, and now his impressionable soul was inspired by the teachings of ahimsa in the land of the Mahatma. Before his mother could say 'United States of America', Kony launched his own Satyagraha. His demands were simple enough. He refused to eat anything till he was served some eggs.

Seema reacted much like the hapless British Empire when an intrepid, loincloth clad figure challenged it. She began the day confident of changing Kony's mind. The arrival of lunchtime witnessed her resorting to threats of dire consequences. But even at that tender age, Kony could sense the power wielded by the victim. He remained adamant. By evening, it was a vanquished Seema who was pleading with her son. No amount of cajoling or inducement by the hapless mother worked. At the end of the day, more than the starving Kony, it was Seema's condition that began to cause disquiet among her hosts.

Perplexed by the drama that was unfolding in her house, Mata ji convened an emergency conference. She was torn asunder between her duty as a hostess and the food habits of a pious housewife as dictated by dharma. After lengthy deliberation, it was decided that the responsibility of the hostess must take precedence.

'I never thought, I'd live to see the day when non-vegetarian food would cross my kitchen's *dehri*. For decades, Pandit ji and his friends tried to persuade me and failed. But this tiny boy...'

'It's all right, Mata ji. You have said on numerous occasions that guests are incarnations of God. An innocent child is more so. Would you begrudge him his heart's desire? Look at him. He hasn't eaten a morsel in the last twelve hours! Neither has Seema. She is on the verge of collapsing with anxiety.'

'I know, I know,' Mata ji muttered. 'As it is, the women of Rameshwar Babu's family are cursed. Not one of them has lived to be sixty. It is her that I'm worried about. The boy is made of sterner stuff. He will be fine by tomorrow. But if something were to happen to her...'

'Nothing will happen to anyone, Mata ji,' Anu was firmly reassuring. 'Varsha has already sent Chedilal to buy two dozen eggs. And some pans too. Indu is having a temporary kitchen set-up in the old cowshed. We haven't kept a cow since I brought Ruby home. Do you remember how Ruby attacked the cow and got a kick in the face for her troubles?'

'I remember perfectly. You and your Ruby were out and out troublemakers. You cost me a good cow. I had to plead with Malati and Chote Bhaiyya to take it to Bageechabad.' Mata ji tried to sound stern but her smile was a giveaway.

'Then it is agreed,' Anu was smiling right back. 'The cowshed will make a comeback as the modern kitchen. You need not worry anymore.'

Within an hour, Kony was celebrating his triumph with an omelette, surrounded by a bevy of admirers. As the womenfolk of the Haveli fretted over him and Mata ji sighed with relief, there arose a new problem.

What is good for the goose holds good for the gander. Her half a dozen grandchildren were not to be outdone. The demands for omelettes, poached, boiled and fried eggs were resounding in every room of the Haveli. Fathers and mothers unsuccessfully tried to reason with obstinate offspring. But Kony's newly discovered version of the Satyagraha found many takers. Before sunset, Mata ji had a taste of the opposition that the *British Empire* encountered as one by one, its colonies overthrew foreign rule. An intelligent woman, she realised that this was an unequal battle that could never be won.

Chedilal went scurrying to bring additional supplies of eggs.

The story should have ended there, but life has an interesting way of making a staid situation piquant.

A good ten days after the arrival of the Prasads and two days and eleven hours after Kony emerged victorious; Mata ji heaved a sigh of relief. Her westernised guests were scheduled to depart in the next forty-eight hours. She had already made preparations for the Haveli to be purified with *gangajal*. Once that Mahatama-esque Kony was out of the picture, she was confident of imposing her will upon her grandchildren and restoring the status quo.

However, this summer was not Mata ji's season for reveling. Fate decided to intervene yet again.

It began with Kony's order for an omelette for breakfast. His mother dutifully carried two eggs to the cowshed-converted into-kitchen where Indu was cooking with Maharani's help. In the presence of two witnesses, Indu cracked the eggs open.

Only to find them empty.

Surprised and a little confused, she profusely apologised to Seema. 'Sometimes our desi eggs tend to be unreliable…Very baffling...but don't you worry, I'll get some more.'

Indu ran back to the fridge in the dining room. In its door, six eggs beamed happily, bought by Chedilal the previous evening. She quickly grabbed two suspiciously lightweight eggs.

Alas! In the kitchen, those turned out to be hollow too. Neither Indu nor Maharani could figure out what was happening! Kony was not helping matters by emptying his lungs out demanding breakfast; while a harried Seema inwardly cursed the day she had entered the Haveli.

Mata ji walked into this hullabaloo after her morning visit to the temple.

'*Arre kya hua*? Why is that boy not being given his eggs? What? The eggs are empty? You both seem to have lost your minds. I wish you would talk some sense, Indu. It is not appropriate for a bahu of this Haveli to utter such rubbish. Gauri, call Varsha and Chedilal at once.'

Varsha, who was in charge of the grocery shopping, was flummoxed. Chedilal was equally bewildered. Both denied knowledge of any wrongdoing, and the consequent responsibility.

'I don't know what happened, Mata ji. I bought the eggs last evening from the shop at the corner. It was like any other day. I can swear that they seemed all right at that time. Do you think there is some evil spirit around?'

Another loud wail from Kony!

'Let's sort this out later,' Mata ji was curt. 'In the meantime, run and get some more eggs. I don't know about you all, but I can both see and hear the devil. Give him the omelette before his mother has another nervous breakdown.'

By afternoon, the Haveli was abuzz with the story of the empty eggs.

Chedilal was enjoying his moment under the spotlight thoroughly. First, he engaged in a heated argument with the shopkeeper. He refused to pay for the eggs. Did anyone pay for an empty bottle or carton? The shopkeeper was also an old hand who gave him an earful and trashed his theories of consumer rights.

Next, on returning to the Haveli, Chedilal loudly recounted his exploits to Varsha. His objective was to garner as much support as possible to prove his innocence. Therefore, when the other ladies joined in, he was extremely gratified. He, of course, pretended to be nonchalant about it. Secretly, he exulted in the attention. Vinu requested him to repeat the full episode before a larger audience—Pandit ji, his sons and Rameshwar Babu. Delighted, he promptly obliged.

'Arrey, Chedilal! Will you only talk the whole day? Or will you use your hands for some work? It is time to cook dinner. Come and help in the kitchen,' Maharani was sweating profusely in the hot kitchen and the picture of Chedilal grinning like a Cheshire cat did not improve her mood.

'Coming, Didi. I'll get some eggs for Kony Bhaiya.'

Aware that all eyes were on him, Chedilal strutted like a peacock towards the refrigerator.

'Hurry up, Chedilal! We don't have the whole day to waste.'

In response to the reprimand from Mata ji, Chedilal further slackened his pace. This time would not come again and he was extracting the last drop of juice from a moment full of potential.

Lo and behold!

'Mata ji, the eggs are light again,' Chedilal observed with a mixture of relish and trepidation.

'What?'

'Mata ji, four of the six eggs that I bought today morning are empty. No, no, Mata ji. I bought them only after checking them painstakingly. I swear they were absolutely fine in the shop.'

'Let me see. Bring them here.'

Vinu, Anu and Sumi crowded around their mother as the others tried to catch a glimpse of the eggs. They need not have bothered. The eggs were passed around, from hand to hand, for closer inspection. Smooth as a baby's skin, the shells glistened palely. Not a single crack could be seen. Mother hen would surely be proud.

Busy examining the eggs, no one noticed when Gauri slumped into a heap. Indu came in from the kitchen, wondering what was taking Chedilal so long and almost tripped over Gauri's unconscious form.

'Chedilal! Run and get some water. Something is wrong with Gauri,' Indu frantically fanned the supine figure with her sari.

'Randhir bhaiyya! Vineet! Come quickly. Take the girl to that room. Under the fan.'

'Place this pillow under her head.'

'Sprinkle some water…Yes, she is coming around.'

'What happened? Why is everyone here?' Gauri woke up in a daze.

'What happened to you, my dear?' Indu's kind voice was soothing.

'I don't know, Bhabhi. One second, I was looking at the eggs. The next—whoosh. The world went black.'

'Why are you so pale? You are shaking all over,' Mata ji quickly placed her palm against Gauri's forehead to check for fever. 'Fortunately, there is no temperature. Perhaps you have exposed yourself to the sun too much. Go and rest for some time in your room.'

Slowly, the group dissipated and went about their chores. Chedilal was dispatched for more eggs.

'And this time, take them straight into the kitchen,' Varsha admonished. Her budget was terribly askew with the unplanned egg procurement and she did not want any more unpleasant surprises.

In the kitchen, Mata ji was supervising the preparations for dinner.

'Maharani, yesterday's chapatis were a little thick. I know, I know, you have to make twenty of them for the dogs. But we can at least feed our guests decent food for two more days. Make sure the chapatis are thin and fluffy tonight. Chedilal, how is that girl now? What timing, I must say! She decides to take ill when we have a house full of guests. Eh? What did you say, Maharani?'

'Now don't get angry, Mata ji. After all, she is a young girl. But don't you think it is too much of a coincidence? The eggshells were hollow. Then Gauri fell senseless. Yesterday the milk boiled over. And the dogs were howling through the night.'

'Even the cat was mewling last night,' Chedilal chimed in. 'I thought it was hungry.'

It earned him a scathing look from Maharani for his efforts.

'What are you trying to say? Speak clearly,' Mata ji's tone was sharp.

Maharani dropped her voice to a whisper so that Mata ji had to strain to hear her. Standing in the corner, Chedilal craned his neck but could barely decipher the exchange.

'I think, there is an evil spirit in the air. It has taken possession of Gauri. Nubile virgins are the most susceptible, Mata ji. We, married women, have our black *mangalsutra* to protect us. I'm sure, she has been stealing the eggs under the influence of the spirit.'

'But why would a spirit come to our Haveli?'

Maharani cleared her throat and continued in an inaudible undertone. 'I'm not sure but I suspect…'

'Speak up, woman! What do you suspect?'

'Do you think it is Rameshwar Babu's wife?' Maharani blurted out.

Mata ji backed away as if she had seen a ghost. She was shaking like a leaf.

'Here, here, Mata ji. Sit down.' Chedilal quickly brought a stool for her to sit on. 'Maharani, stop your jabbering. Why are you putting all these silly ideas in Mata ji's head?'

With great acrobatic skill, he had maneuvered to get within hearing distance and caught Maharani's last words.

Maharani sniffled, 'I did not volunteer anything on my own. It was only when Mata ji asked me that I spoke. You think it's all hogwash. Well, we shall see. Do *you* have any explanation for the hollow eggs?'

Mata ji was as white as a sheet. When she spoke, her voice was not quite steady.

'I cannot take a chance, Chedilal. Go, get Pandit Bholenath.'

'But the dinner?'

'Go! We will manage without you. Hurry!'

By nightfall, the entire household at the Haveli was in turmoil. In every room, the discussion revolved around the mystery of the missing eggs and the frail Gauri. Various theories were postulated but none could explain the happenings satisfactorily. After dinner, as the family members and the guests relaxed in the lawns Mata ji paced restlessly in the driveway. The sweet-scented parijat failed to calm her overwrought nerves today.

'Why has Chedilal not returned with Pandit Bholenath?' she murmured under her breath.

As if in answer to her prayers, Chedilal sauntered in.

'You rascal! Why are you sauntering in like a bride? And where is Bholenath? I've been waiting for ages.'

'Pandit Bholenath can't come.' In the face of Mata ji's verbal assault, Chedilal's speech quickened with his steps. 'He has gone to his village. He shall return the day after tomorrow.'

'What?' Mata ji collapsed in a chair. 'What should we do now?'

'But why did you send for Pandit Bholenath, Mata ji? Isn't he the *ojha*? Why do we need an ojha?' Chhaya was at her side.

'Shh! Lower your voice. We need not tell the whole world about it.'

'About what, Mata ji?' Chhaya was insistent.

'I think there is an evil spirit in the house.'

Chhaya involuntarily took a step back. Mata ji continued, 'Yes, I am convinced. How else do you explain these strange events?'

'Mata ji, you have been listening to Maharani again,' Vinu joined them.

At Mata ji's flushed visage, Vinu pressed her advantage home. 'As I said, there is no spirit around, evil or otherwise. It is a case of too many people and an overworked help. Gauri has been worked to the bone in the last ten days. She was exhausted, poor thing. Is it a crime to faint in your regime?'

'But what about the eggs?'

'Well, let us check right now.'

Vinu strode into the house with aplomb and opened the fridge where only a few hours ago Chedilal had deposited a dozen eggs. With a confident look, she picked up the first egg in the rack, only to freeze mid-motion. And then she dropped it from her nerveless fingers with a shriek.

All eyes turned to the cracked shell on the floor for confirmation. The egg did not disappoint. It was empty; a trickle of thick fluid oozed out, residual proof that at some point it was a receptacle of life.

'Is everything alright?' Seema had come in to check. 'I heard someone scream.'

'Oh yes. Nothing to fret about. Vinu saw a cockroach. She has always been scared of them,' Chhaya improvised wildly.

'By the way, Mata ji, your brother has sent some ripe, juicy mangoes.' It was Chedilal providing the much-needed diversion in an awkward situation.

'Mangoes!'

Seema, Chhaya and Vinu shouted in unison with childlike glee, momentarily forgetting the disagreeable circumstances they were in.

'Arrey, why didn't you say it all this time? Now don't blabber. Go and get the mangoes inside.'

The hamper, laden with ripe Dussehri from Mata ji's village in Bageechabad, received a warm welcome—one reserved for blue-blooded guests. It was a huge wicker basket, filled to the brim with sweet-smelling mangoes. Its aroma was sufficient to draw all the members around the table and diverted the attention of the family from the unfortunate occurrences of the day.

Very soon, the crop of mangoes this year had replaced the hollow eggs as the topic for discussion.

Not for everyone, though.

In Mata ji's room, there was a whispered parley between Chhaya, Vinu and Mata ji. They decided to summon Pandit Bholenath on his return. Gauri was definitely afflicted with something, ethereal or temporal. She was to be denied entry into the house for a few days, at least till Bholenath arrived.

'All this is very good, Mata ji. But what if there is nothing to be exorcised? I've seen some of Bholenath's victims. I'm not sure a person has *anything* left in them after Bholenath finishes. The dhobi's daughter visited him last year. She received such a thrashing that she was bedridden for weeks. Sometimes I wonder whether the so-called *evil spirit* isn't actually a lot kinder than him! Gauri is an orphan but that means our responsibility towards her well-being is also much greater.'

'What are you trying to say?' Mata ji was belligerent. 'Of course, I treat Gauri as my own daughter. Okay, almost as a sister's daughter. This is for her good.'

'You may say so Mata ji, but I don't like Bholenath. He is a sadist and enjoys torturing his victims,' Chhaya shuddered as she recalled the condition of the dhobi's daughter.

'Maybe things will be different tomorrow and we needn't call Bholenath. Isn't it, Mata ji?' Vinu pleaded.

Mata ji reluctantly nodded in agreement.

'I'll visit the Hanuman temple and offer a prasad of 151 rupees if this trouble goes away. Now I wish we all wake up tomorrow morning to find the eggs intact!'

'Ameen,' intoned Chhaya and Vinu together.

'Ameen,' Mata ji disapprovingly parroted.

***

If you believe in something, it exists. You can see and hear things if you believe they are there.

Nothing could have been more apposite to the situation in the Haveli at that juncture. The strong belief that there was a phantom in the house gave it a greater credence than its actual sighting would probably have.

Moreover, like humans, not all spirits are alike. If some evil spirits were attacking Mata ji's family, there were also the good ones lurking in the corners of the ancient Haveli, watching over its inhabitants. There had to be, for *someone* heard Vinu's prayers. As the morning dawned bright and early, Chhaya rushed to the refrigerator to check on the eggs that were placed in it the previous night.

Wonder of wonders! All the eight eggs were intact!

Throughout the day, Vinu or Chhaya kept checking the eggs like suspicious mother hens. By evening, there was a feeling of reassurance that the danger had passed. They suggested that Bholenath should wait for another day. A relieved Mata ji fulfilled her promise to the powers that be. To Pandit ji's astonishment, she insisted on distributing prasad to the beggars outside the Hanuman temple. On the second day, too, normalcy prevailed.

By the third day, it was time to bid farewell to Rameshwar Babu and his flock.

'How can I ever thank you, Mata ji? You have been the perfect hostess—hospitable and caring. You opened your doors and your heart to my family. You went the extra mile and broke your vow for the sake of my grandson. I'll never be able to express my gratitude to you adequately. Please forgive us for the inconvenience we have caused you.'

Mata ji blushed at these very publicly and effusively articulated words. She felt a trifle ashamed as she recalled the occasions when she had felt less than charitable towards her guests. For the first time in her life, she was tongue-tied. After savouring her discomfort for a few moments, Pandit ji stepped in to rescue her.

'Not at all, Ramu. You are embarrassing us. We have done nothing more than is expected. I am sure that you would have done the same for us. We thoroughly enjoyed your company. The youngsters got a chance to know each other. I hope you will stay with us on your next visit too, which ought to be sooner.'

'You bet, we will.' Kony's enthusiastic shout was all the endorsement needed as the two families, bound together by the silken threads of friendship, parted ways.

As for the enigma of the hollow eggs, it would have remained a mystery forever, intriguing those associated with it. Except that truth has a tendency to emerge in the most incredible and sudden ways. In this case, it came in the form of a letter in Vinu's elegant handwriting after a few months.

Dear Mata ji,

Sadar Pranam! Obeisance!

I hope your backache is cured now. Did you use the oil that I sent you with Hariprasad? It was from Kerala and is supposed to be miraculous for relieving back pain. As Hari might have mentioned to you, I got this bottle especially for you from my neighbour. Mr Tyagi has recently been transferred to Kerala but he visits his family here every month. If you found the oil useful, I could ask him to bring another vial the next time he comes.

The real reason why I'm writing to you, though, is not the ayurvedic oil. I'm sure, you would recall the incident of the hollow eggs during the summer break. We never did find out the truth at that time. Well, I discovered it yesterday!

Please accept my apologies in advance for what I'm going to share in the next few paragraphs. Further, if you are reading this letter in someone's presence, move to another room and read this alone.

Last night, Sonu and Monu demanded eggs for dinner. I flatly refused as neither you nor their dadi has allowed cooking of non-vegetarian food in the house. I've observed the same ritual all my life though, to tell you the truth, I've never really understood how food is related to the purity of the mind and soul. Anyway, let me not digress from the main point.

As I said, I rejected the very thought of cooking eggs in my kitchen. Despite my opposition, they went and got half a dozen eggs from the market. I, too, waited patiently to see how they would enter my kitchen. I was determined to fight to the finish! After all, unless these values are inculcated at a young age, they will not follow them later in life.

To my utter surprise and horror, the boys made no move to use the kitchen. They washed the eggs and then proceeded to puncture the shells with a needle. With pursed lips, they sucked all the contents of the eggs. It was over in a minute. I was too stunned to react. By the time I got my voice back, they had devoured all the eggs. There, lying on my sunmica table top were six glistening eggshells. Only they were emptied and sucked hollow, as we had discovered this back in summer.

The boys confessed that they had been doing this during the summer without realising what they were setting into motion. Apparently, they did not enjoy the food that was served (too many *vegetables and greens!) and eggs were in short supply. Varsha was balancing the budget while catering to guests and family members alike. As the eldest children, Sonu and Monu naturally got the short end of the stick. Whenever there was a cutback, it was from their share. Soon, they devised a way of reclaiming what they believed was rightfully theirs.*

Mata ji, do you remember that the eggs stopped getting hollow soon after the mangoes arrived? At that time, we never made the connection. Now I see it as clear as daylight. Once the mangoes came, they lost interest in eggs and feasted upon the fruit.

I did not know whether to laugh or cry when I heard their story. On one hand, I was glad that the enigma of the hollow eggs had been solved. On the other, when I recall how we were planning to call Pandit Bholenath and hand Gauri over to him…

I've never felt more ashamed, Mata ji. I beg you not to allow Maharani to fill your head with such hocus-pocus ever again. You must promise me, Mata ji. We are role models for our children. If they come to know what we were thinking and planning, they would never forgive us.

Do keep this to yourself, if you can. Even Chhaya Bhabhi must not know. We both are guilty of a grave sin and we must atone for it by showering greater affection on Gauri.

To begin with, buy her some new clothes and give her the sweater that I have sent in the parcel. I knitted it for her. But this will be a minuscule part of the penance that we both must do, beginning from now.

Your loving daughter,

Vinu.

THE MISSING BREAKFAST

Breakfast time! What else could be a better way to fathom the truest nature of filial bonds in a household? At this hour of the day, when all and sundry are making a mad dash, tempers are frayed and words are shorn of pretense. Each one is in a race against some imaginary or not so-imaginary clock. And just like any other contest, no one wants to end up last. They push and nudge in a bid to stay ahead.

Panditji's Haveli was not an exception.

Each morning, unfailingly, before the sun emerged from its soft, wooly blanket of clouds, the day commenced.

'Where have all of you disappeared? Gauri? Chedilal? Where are you? The dogs need to be let out. Have you become deaf? Can't you hear them howling?' Mata ji's voice echoed from the nooks and corners of the Haveli.

'Oh no! Why does Mata ji start so early in the morning?' Sumeet groaned, desperately trying to shut out her voice by burrowing deeper inside the covers.

'I wish I had the luxury of turning over and going back to sleep. Unfortunately, that is not a privilege accorded to the bahus here,' Chhaya was bitter as she forced her feet into the cold, rubber slippers.

'Indu!' Mata ji was banging on the door. 'Come on. It's time to cook breakfast. Have you finished taking a bath? Good. Get started then. And listen, I'm going to the temple. Make sure that everything is done by the time I return.'

'Everything' is an innocent word. It can mean many things and yet nothing. At that juncture, it meant—release the dogs for their morning run in the lawns, place a jug of warm water on the dining table for Pandit ji, collect the newspaper from the gate and place it near Pandit ji's chair, sweep the temple in the courtyard and offer fresh water and flowers at the altar, peel the almonds soaked the previous night for the children and peel the garlic pods for Pandit ji (in that order otherwise the smell of garlic would spoil the almonds), prepare the morning tea, send the steaming cups to the still-sleepy occupants in their rooms, prepare breakfast and fill the tiffin boxes for the six children in the house, ensure that water in a large vat in the courtyard was simmering over firewood so that the children could bathe and reach school on time, prepare breakfast for the ten adult members of the family, the four dogs and the three helps; all this while responding to shouts of 'Indu, where is my tea?' or 'Indu, why haven't you warmed up Pinki's milk?'

To an ordinary mortal this would have been daunting. It definitely appeared unnerving to Indu at the beginning. However, with the passage of time, it became child's play. Frederick Winslow Taylor would have been proud to see her apply his principles of scientific management as she devised her own pattern—on the way to the gate to collect the morning paper, she would gather the flowers for the temple; while preparing the tea, she would give instructions to Maharani about what to put together for breakfast and tiffin. Separate tasks were assigned to Gauri, Chedilal and Maharani. She was everywhere, with everyone, with a smile here and a pat there, a picture of effortless efficiency.

'Gauri, drink your tea or it will get cold. I know you have to pack the tiffin. It's okay. There is time. Take a minute and sip the tea.'

Indu thrust the warm cup into a grateful Gauri's hand while she herself took over the task of packing the tiffin boxes.

'Ahh. Something smells good. What is in the tiffin, *Chachi*?' Young Guddu was the first one to come to the kitchen every morning, partly because he loved food and partly because he liked Indu Chachi who always gave him an extra helping if he visited her in the kitchen.

'*Pakoris*, dear. You like them, don't you?'

'Yummy!'

'Is everything alright?' Mata ji had returned from the temple.

'Yes, Mata ji. Pandit ji has taken his water and garlic. The children have finished their bath, eaten breakfast and are off to school. Chedilal has gone to see them off at the gate. Breakfast for the others will be ready in a few minutes. Would you like a cup of tea?'

'Have the dogs been fed?' Mata ji detested four legged creatures. She had fought like a tigress to oppose their entry into the Haveli. Over the years, though, she had acquired the zeal of a neo-convert and had taken the pets into the fold of her family.

'Maharani is making their rotis.'

'Okay. Make a cup of tea for me once *you've* given them their food. For Indu, it is you, the bahu of the Haveli who must feed the dogs. Don't ask Maharani to do it on your behalf. Never.'

Indu was quite used to this lecture every morning. With a demure smile, she acquiesced and went about finishing her chores.

By the time the 'grandfather clock' in the drawing room chimed 10, Sundar was ready with the car. Pandit ji, in his impeccable achkan and Nehru cap, set out for another day of battle in Court. He left for his chambers along with Sumeet and Randheer. The car dropped them and returned exactly at 12:30 to carry their lunch back.

Varsha lovingly packed the food for the three men and handed it over to Sundar.

Each day, the two of them had the same exchange:

'Did you drop Pandit ji and Sumeet Bhaiyya, Sundar?'

'Of course, Bhabhi. Randheer Bhaiyya too, even though you never ask about him,' Sundar smirked as Varsha blushed.

'Dot on time. Every day, as the clock strikes 10:30, our car enters the court. Among the lawyers, it is said that one can wind the clock by Sundar's car, Bhabhi,' he proudly announced.

'All right, all right, now stop your lecture and take their lunch. And mind you, go straight to the court. Don't waste time loitering here and there.'

'Loitering? Do you think Pandit ji would have kept me all these years if I were the kind to loaf around?'

Sundar would pretend to be deeply offended. In reality, he enjoyed this daily repartee with Varsha. Sometimes he felt sorry for the women in Pandit ji's Haveli—intelligent creatures, locked up in the mansion. Quite unlike some of the young women he saw in the court. He firmly believed that Pandit ji's daughters-in-law would make far worthy successors than either Randheer or Sumeet.

One day he plucked up enough courage to ask Varsha, 'Bhabhi, why don't you pursue an LLB degree? Then you and Randheer Bhaiyya could practice together. You'd make a fine lawyer.'

'*Chhee*, Sundar! What will Pandit ji think? Women from the Haveli do not work outside the house. Are the men here not capable of fending for their families that their wives have to look for jobs?'

'Don't blame Pandit ji if you are not interested in studying law, Bhabhi,' Sundar stoutly defended his master. 'He has always favoured the idea of women stepping out of the house to carve out an independent identity. Haven't you seen how considerate he is towards Suhasini Didi? He made her his junior when no other senior advocate was willing to give her an opportunity to practice. He treats her no differently from his sons. Be that as it may, who am I to advise you? I'm sure you know better, so I'll be minding my own business.'

'Indeed, that will be better,' Varsha was dismissive. The audacity of the old rascal! He was a shrewd fellow. How in the world did he guess that she harboured the dream of studying law and practising in the court one day? If Mata ji were to hear of it, she would ensure that Varsha was assigned to kitchen duties for the rest of her life.

'Has Sundar left? Call him back quickly,' Madhu was gasping.

'What happened?'

'Indu has fainted. She sat down for a second on the dining table and the next minute, she slumped over, unconscious. Call

Sundar. He must fetch Vineet from the court. Someone has to take her to the doctor.'

'Oh my God! He has already left. What do we do now?'

'I'll send Chedilal to find a rickshaw. There is no time to waste. The two of us can take her to Dr Jain's clinic. I've been there a couple of times. It's not too far. Hurry!'

***

By the next morning, the small storm had transformed into a full-blown blizzard. In the Haveli, everything was at sixes and sevens. Tasks that appeared like a piece of cake with Indu at the helm, were unmitigated disasters in her absence. Chhaya took on the responsibility of the kitchen with Maharani, Varsha of the breakfast and kids' zone and Madhu of the bathing arrangements.

'*Taiji*, my milk is too hot.'

'I hate porridge, Mummy. Why don't you make poha like Indu Chachi?'

'Varsha! Where are my garlic pods?'

The three ladies somehow got the children off to school. As they heaved a sigh of relief, the next barrage of demands arrived—

'Madhu, when will I get my tea?'

'Where is the newspaper?'

'Has no one let the dogs out? They are howling like banshees.'

'I'll get breakfast this time, Badi Bhabhi. You handle the dining table,' Varsha escaped to the sanctuary of the kitchen without giving Chhaya a chance to reply. 'At least there is peace in the kitchen, Maharani. You can't imagine how spoilt these children have become.'

'I don't have to, Bhabhi. I see them every morning,' Maharani snickered. 'While you sip your chai under your quilt, Indu Bhabhi and I are here with them.'

'Me too,' chirped Gauri. 'Don't worry. I'm sure, everyone is praying for Indu Bhabhi's quick recovery. She will return in a few days and then matters will be like before.'

'What did the doctor say, Bhabhi?'

Before Varsha could respond, the omniscient Gauri was ready. 'She has some sort of fever. I forgot the name… Doctor said rest for five or six days will make her as good as new.'

'Well, I guess we all must learn to cope till then,' Maharani was stoical.

'You, young women are good for nothing,' Mata ji stomped into the kitchen. 'Poor Pandit ji has been staring at his empty plate since ages. Where is his toast?'

'I sent it ten minutes ago, Mata ji. Gauri served it.'

On Varsha's enquiring look, Gauri nodded vigorously.

'Yes, Mata ji! I kept the buttered toast on the table.'

'I may be getting on in age, but I'm definitely not blind. There is an empty plate on the table, young lady. So, stop telling tales and get on with toasting the bread.'

Thoroughly bewildered, but thinking it wiser not to belabour the point, Varsha started preparing another batch of toasted bread with butter. All human beings are permitted some foible. Buttered bread was Pandit ji's.

Every morning, Chedilal got a freshly baked loaf of bread from the nearby bakery. From this loaf, four slices of bread were toasted for him. Neither a slice more nor a slice less. Though he was careful to consume very little ghee otherwise, he enjoyed his hot toast with a dollop of butter. The bread, soaked with soft molten butter, augured a perfect day. Over the years, Indu had recognised his penchant for toast and ensured that his breakfast was served just the way he liked it.

In the dining room, Pandit ji sat and stared blankly at the empty plate with thoughts chasing each other in his head. That chit of a girl, Indu, had taken the entire burden of running the house on her delicate shoulders. Mata ji did not realise how fortunate she was to have her. Or perhaps she did. She *did* have an uncanny sense of delegating responsibility. Even if it meant one person shouldering most of it! The next few days would be interesting, to say the least; particularly for the pampered members of this family. Though he had never thought of himself as spoilt before, he realised that he had begun to expect things as per his liking. He was surely missing his tailor-made breakfast.

On this wistful note, Pandit ji rose and left for his morning ablutions.

As he stepped over the threshold, Gauri rushed in with a plate of buttered toast. Not espying Pandit ji anywhere, she placed the toast on the table and left for the next errand.

Every few minutes, Gauri would zig-zag through the dining hall on some chore or the other. She checked on Pandit ji's breakfast: the toast lay untouched.

After about three quarters of an hour, she returned to find Pandit ji ready and seated at the table, staring irately at the empty plate.

'Highly unusual that Pandit ji has eaten eight slices and is still waiting for more. Perhaps there is something amiss with his digestion. But I am in no position to tell him to watch his diet,' Gauri hesitantly waited for a word from him.

When Pandit ji continued to eye his plate yearningly, she felt a flood of pity.

'Poor old man! I should not count how many pieces of bread he eats.'

She turned to Pandit ji and enquired solicitously, '*Kya Hua*, Pandit ji? Would you like me to get some more bread for you?'

'More bread?' Pandit ji was apoplectic. 'A man cannot get two pieces of bread in his own house, and you, my girl, are asking me if I can get *more* bread. Are you in your right mind?'

On hearing raised voices, Mata ji rushed into the room. No one had seen the mild-mannered Pandit ji in such a rage.

Spotting his wife, Pandit ji directed his ire at her.

'And you, Shakuntala! You are supposed to run this house. Is this how you do it? I have been waiting for my breakfast for two hours. Every time I come to this table, I see an empty plate. What kind of a house is this? No, I do not want to hear excuses any more. Chedilal! Tell Sundar to get the car. I'm leaving for the court right away.'

Pandit ji stormed out of the house, a stunned audience watching his retreating back.

Not for long.

Ayurveda believes that each of us is composed of different elements. Mata ji's spirit was most likely made of copper. She conducted things with great speed and undiminished quantum.

'Varsha!' she hollered. 'Why wasn't Pandit ji given his breakfast? Didn't I tell you to do so?'

Varsha broke into a sweat.

'Of course, you did, Mata ji. As per your directions, I immediately sent another plate of buttered toast. Gauri brought it. You can ask Maharani.'

Sensing trouble, Gauri placed herself at a safe distance from Mata ji.

'Has the cat got your tongue, you wretched girl? Speak up! What have you done with the toast?'

'I kept it on the table, Mata ji.' The words were drawn out in a choked whisper.

'Then who ate it? Did the walls swallow it? Or did the floor suddenly open up and the toast sank into *Mother Earth*'s embrace?'

These were rhetorical questions and the onlookers wisely realised that silence was the only answer expected of them. After a while, with no response from any quarter, Mata ji crumpled into a heap on the chair.

'It is my fault. I should have seen that this was bound to happen one day.'

Everyone watched her nervously, as if she was a man-eater who would spring on its prey any moment.

The grandfather clock ticked loudly and intrepidly. It had witnessed worse scenes.

Suddenly Mata ji's face brightened.

'Why didn't I think of this earlier? Chedilal, go at once and fetch Chandra Prakash.'

Chedilal was delighted to leave the emotionally charged Haveli for some fresh air. With the alacrity of a teenager, he rushed out. The others watched his escape with disgust-laced envy.

'Should we prepare lunch, Mata ji?' Chhaya almost whispered.

'I would rather starve than eat something cooked by you, my dear. As for the rest of you, I couldn't care less. In any case, today is *amavasya*. Perhaps it will be a good idea for you to fast.'

Though Mata ji walked out after her smart retort to her good-for-nothing daughters-in-law, she was deeply perturbed. Part of her was ashamed that Pandit ji had left the house without eating a morsel. She should have looked after his meal herself. She wondered where he would eat now. Most likely at Sharma Chaat Bhandaar. He had a weakness for chaat and it was his favourite joint. Except that after every visit, he was left with a bout of acidity. Sighing deeply, she checked to ensure that there was medicine for that particular malady in the house.

Another part of her mind was furious at everyone, including Indu. The girl should have taken better care. At Dr Jain's clinic, she confessed that she was running a temperature for the last three days. Lack of rest and medicines had caused her illness to aggravate. If only Indu had told her earlier! This could have been avoided. There is nothing that a dose of homeopathic medicine, taken on time, cannot cure. Things would never have come to such a pass. Indu knew very well that the rest of them—Chhaya, Varsha and Madhu—could not be relied upon. It was typical of her to be so irresponsible!

As usual, *she* would have to do something. Which was why she had sent for the old hand, Chandra Prakash. He was a man worth his weight in gold, generally invited to manage households during weddings or when a large gathering of guests was expected. Only the well-off could afford his services. But he was worth every paisa and Mata ji was convinced that this was a crisis that required extraordinary measures.

In any event, if Pandit ji wanted his perfectly buttered toast, he ought to be prepared to pay a price for it.

She smiled at her own wit and walked out to the lawn to wait for Chandra Prakash.

***

'Oh God! When will Indu recover, Varsha?'

'Badi Bhabhi! My feet hurt. I've never stood for so long in my whole life.'

'Only your feet! I can feel all the two hundred and fifty bones in my body.'

'Not two-fifty, Badi Bhabhi. There are about two hundred of them.'

'Whatever. If this continues, I'm leaving for my parents' house, Varsha.'

'Really? Who do you think is going to feed your brats and pander to your husband's whims and fancies then?'

'Speaking of children, our offspring could do with some disciplining. They have become too demanding and ill-mannered.'

'They are taking after their fathers. I asked Vineet to let out the dogs and he refused saying that he was getting late. Can you believe it?'

'Shhh, here comes Mata ji.'

'Chhaya, I have spoken to Chandra Prakash. He has agreed to help us from tomorrow morning. As soon as he comes, ask him to make a list of groceries and essential items that are needed. Explain to him the details of breakfast. Make sure that there is no mix-up about Pandit ji's toast tomorrow.' Mata ji's warning brooked no argument. She stormed out without waiting for an answer.

'Phew! She was furious. It seems Pandit ji is extremely cross.'

'I don't know but I intend to keep out of his way till the situation improves.'

***

Chandra Prakash's arrival was heralded with great joy. He accepted the welcome coolly with a self-assurance that would have seemed akin to arrogance had his hosts not been blinded by relief and gratitude.

With supreme efficiency, he got the kitchen running in no time; barking directions to Gauri, Chedilal and Maharani, while Chhaya and Varsha stood on the side and watched in awe.

'Has the tiffin been packed, Gauri? Good. Chedilal, go and keep these bowls on the table. Bhabhi,' Chandra Prakash summoned Varsha who scampered towards him obediently, 'Could you make sure that the children eat their breakfast? Yes, it will indeed be better if you waited in the dining room. Maharani, is the tea ready? No? Hurry up, please. Badi Bhabhi, could you please tell me how many parathas are to be made for breakfast? Thank you. If you could sit right there and guide me.

Yes, that is fine. You can answer my questions from there.'

His terse instructions echoed in the Haveli and the Awasthi clan heaved a sigh of relief to finally have someone in charge.

Yet, due to his unfamiliarity with the Haveli's routine, he could not be expected to match Indu on day one itself.

'Varsha Bhabhi, you know I don't like so much sugar in my tea. Ughhh.'

'It's all right, Vineet. I'll get you another cup. Chandra Prakash is new, you know.'

'How is Indu Bhabhi now?'

'She is mending well. Should be back on her feet in a week, I think.'

'*Ishwar Kripa Karein*'

Thus, even with Chandra Prakash's help, not everything was as smooth as one would have wished. And that includes Pandit ji's toast!

'Listen, girl. I've been waiting for a long time. If I wait any more, I'll be late for work. You make sure that you get my toast and place it right here.' Pandit ji spoke slowly and punctuated his words with actions so that there could be no misunderstanding.

'Ji, ji, Pandit ji.' Gauri's eyes were as wide as saucers and her voice shook. Mata ji's ominous threats had worked their magic.

Thus, after half an hour, when she brought the toast, she proceeded to guard it like the Crown Jewels.

9:10, 9:20… Almost time for Pandit ji to don his achkan and arrive. Gauri checked again on the toast. Safe, though a bit cold and soggy! She felt a furry body brush past her. It was Ruby, Pandit ji's favourite dog.

'Ruby, Ruby,' Gauri cooed, bending down to pet her, and then thought better as Ruby bared her teeth. She only allowed Pandit ji to touch her. 'What do you want? Do you want to go out? Poor baby, we forgot your breakfast. Wait. I'll ask Didi to make you some.'

She found Maharani busy kneading some dough in the kitchen.

'Didi, we forgot the dogs' food. They are hungry. Will you make some rotis quickly? Mata ji will be very cross if she discovers that they haven't been fed.'

'Yes, your *Highness*. Thank you. You were thc only one left to issue orders to me. Now the list is complete. Can't you see I'm preparing dough for their rotis?'

The extra work load and constant tension was making everyone irritable.

'Well, I've done my bit. Don't blame me if Mata ji gives you a piece of her mind. Now I must return and wait for Pandit ji to have his toast.'

The sight that met Gauri's eyes on returning to the dining hall made her blood run cold. Pandit ji was morosely staring at an empty plate.

Not knowing what to do, she burst into loud wails.

'I swear I kept the toast here, Pandit ji. I even stood by watching it. It was right here, as you directed. But then, Ruby came. She was hungry....'

Pandit ji decided not to wait to hear the rest of her rambling story. Resigned to another morning at Sharma Chaat Bhandaar and an added dose of Lomotil in the evening, he picked up his brass-headed walking stick and marched out.

'Is that the car? Has Pandit ji left? Someone ask him to...' Mata ji stopped in her tracks. In a second she fathomed what had happened; Gauri howling and shedding copious tears; Chandra Prakash looking bewildered, while Chhaya, Varsha, Chedilal and Maharani looked torn between fear and surprise.

'Quit making a fool of yourself, girl. Tell me what happened.'

Hiccupping, coughing and occasionally bursting into a fresh spate of tears, Gauri narrated her ordeal.

'Okay. All of you leave. Chhaya and Varsha, I want to have a word with both of you.'

Once they were alone, Mata ji did not beat around the bush.

'I had asked you to supervise the meals with Maharani's assistance, Chhaya. As the eldest daughter-in-law of this house, you enjoy certain privileges. You must understand that they come with some responsibilities. The head of the family has left the house without any food for the second day. What do you have to say about that?'

Chhaya's eyes moistened and her voice choked. 'I'm sorry, Mata ji. I was ...'

'I do not want to hear any explanations,' Mata ji's voice cut through like a whip. 'You have failed miserably. Varsha, from tomorrow, you will be at the helm of the kitchen and Chhaya, you will supervise the meals in the dining room. Go now.'

Feeling like naughty schoolgirls dismissed by the principal, the two women tiptoed out.

'What is happening, Badi Bhabhi?'

'I don't know. But I don't care to be labeled a failure.' Chhaya's voice cracked.

'Don't worry, Badi Bhabhi,' Varsha squeezed her arm comfortingly. 'We will find out. Do you think it's the handiwork of that girl Gauri? She is really fond of Indu. Could she be causing this trouble to get back at us? After all, we were never pleasant to Indu or to her.'

'Of course! Why didn't I think of this before? She literally worships the ground Indu walks on. You are absolutely right. You are a genius, Varsha.'

'No, no, Badi Bhabhi. The truth is that I have been mulling over this since yesterday. You see, Gauri is the only one who could have done this. I have a proposition. Let us catch her red-handed tomorrow. Then…'

'Then, I'll take great pleasure in skinning her alive. Little witch. Putting up such a splendid performance before the entire Haveli today; her innocent face will not deceive me anymore!'

***

By night time, a pall of gloom had descended upon the Haveli. Family members were short-tempered while the helpers were wary. There was a perceptible sense of fear in the air. At the dining table, the children were subdued. Young Guddu took one look at his mother's scowling face and decided against asking for another serving. Once dinner was over, Chhaya and Varsha went for a stroll outside the Haveli. Under the shade of the parijat trees, they finalised their war plan for the next day.

'We must proceed exactly as discussed. Once caught in the act, the girl will have no defense.'

'Don't worry, Badi Bhabhi. There will be no mistake. Tomorrow will be the *Judgment Day* for her.'

***

In contrast to the other days of the week, Sundays were leisurely and slow-paced in Pandit ji's Haveli. There was no school or the court to rush to, and Mata ji's mandir timings were more relaxed. At the appointed hour, Varsha set the ball rolling.

'Gauri! Come and take Pandit ji's breakfast.'

'Should I take it, Bhabhi?' Chedilal's unctuous offer could not have come at a worse time.

'Nahi, nahi, Chedilal. You go and check the water. The weather has turned warm; so make sure that it isn't too hot. Madhu will bring the young brigade for their bath any minute. Ah! There you are, Gauri. Take the buttered toast. It's time for Pandit ji's breakfast.'

Standing in the dining hall, Chhaya was waiting for this moment. She heard Varsha's summons for Gauri and braced herself.

'Just on time, Gauri. I spotted Pandit ji going to his room. He will be here in a minute. Place the toast on the table and wait right here. It's your responsibility to keep an eye on it. Under no circumstances should you leave it unattended,' Chhaya cautioned Gauri.

She then withdrew to her vantage point near the grandfather clock. From that position she had a clear view of the room and the passage leading to the kitchen, while remaining unobserved.

The clock ticked loudly. Nine chimes followed. No signs of Pandit ji.

'He hasn't eaten breakfast for three days in a row now. Is it possible that he has given up on us and thinks there will be none served today either? Should I call him? But that would mean leaving Gauri unsupervised.'

Chhaya cast a quick glance at Gauri. Wearing an expression of extreme boredom, she stood near Pandit ji's chair, gazing sullenly at the plate of warm toast. She was literally keeping an eye on the plate!

'Hurry up, Pandit ji. In another minute…'

Chhaya's musings were cut short.

'Aaaaaaa! Mummmmyyy! Bachao!'

The blood-curdling scream galvanised Chhaya into action. Pinki was shouting for help. The sound came from the garden. In a heartbeat, she was sprinting out of the house towards Pinki.

'Mummyyyy….'

Pinki cowered under the mango tree, surrounded by three muscular monkeys baring their teeth at her.

As Chhaya charged at them, they switched their attention from Pinki to her. Terror rose within her. In her haste, she had forgotten to bring anything to tackle them with.

'Bhabhi, don't worry. I've got a lathi.' Out of nowhere, Chedilal materialised at her side. He had anticipated the situation better and was armed with a stick.

In a few seconds order was restored. The monkeys were chased away. Pinki was rescued and safely ensconced in her mother's arms.

As Chhaya comforted the sobbing child, she heaved a sigh of relief.

'You had a narrow escape today, Pinki. Thank God, they didn't hurt you. It's okay now. Don't cry. Were you very scared? Aren't you a brave girl to shout for help? That was a sensible thing to do.'

As they moved towards the house, Chhaya found Gauri following them.

'Come, Pinki. Let's go and gather some flowers. We can make a garland for your dolls today,' offered Gauri.

'Gauri! What are you doing here?'

'Uh, Badi Bhabhi, uh, I ran out on hearing Pinki scream. I stayed a little away as you know I'm scared of monkeys but I...'

'No, no. That's all right. But if you are here who is watching over Pandit ji's toast?'

The words had hardly left her mouth when Gauri scurried into the house like a hare.

'What happened, Mummy? Why did Gauri run away like that? Won't she help me pick flowers?'

'Of course, she will, darling. In a minute. But you need to be careful with monkeys in this season. Now let's go inside. I need to check if Pandit ji has eaten his breakfast.'

In the dining hall, Gauri's stricken face was all the confirmation Chhaya needed. That and the empty plate on the table.

Footsteps.

'Gauri, you fool! I told you to watch over the breakfast. Why were you so careless?' Chhaya hissed angrily.

With her eyes brimming like two over-filled pools, Gauri barely choked out an answer.

'Pinki…'

Chhaya softened marginally.

'Now run and get another batch. Pandit ji is coming. I'll keep him engaged in conversation for a while. Quickly!'

Gauri acted like a drowning person who has been thrown a lifeline. She ran pell-mell towards the kitchen even as Pandit ji walked in.

'Good morning, Chhaya. Are things under control today?'

'Better,' she wryly replied. 'Chandra Prakash is a tremendous help.'

'I'm glad to hear that. I am sure you realise that we are spending an enormous amount of money on him. How is Indu?'

'Convalescing. Dr Jain said she should be back on her feet in two or three days.'

'That should bring some cheer to the family. So, will I get my breakfast today or do I have to visit Sharma's again?'

'No, no, Pandit ji. Chandra Prakash is preparing it just as you like it. Ah! Here comes Gauri.'

Pandit ji rubbed his hands together in comical relief.

'Waah! A perfect beginning to the day. You know, even Sharma's chaat cannot beat the taste of warm butter soaking into fresh bread. Mmm.'

Mata ji was grinning like a cheshire cat. 'Chalo, let him enjoy his breakfast.'

***

In the kitchen, Varsha was waiting expectantly.

'Did it go as per plan, Badi Bhabhi?'

Chhaya nodded, 'Except for a minor glitch.'

She quickly narrated the incident with the monkeys.

'Good. Now let's show them that we are the daughters-in-law of Advocate Pandit Dinanath Awasthi.'

***

'Pandit ji, we have a request.'

He sighed in resignation. A man could not have an unhurried browsing of the newspaper on other days. Sunday was the only day when he permitted himself this luxury. However, if Varsha and Chhaya were determined to interrupt his reverie, then so be it. Pandit ji folded the newspaper, pushed his moon-shaped spectacles down on his nose and gazed over them at his daughters-in-law.

Varsha cleared her throat.

'You may have noticed that there has been some disorder regarding your breakfast, Pandit ji.'

Pandit ji's eyes almost popped out. Disorder! That was an understatement. For three days in a row he had to leave on an empty stomach in the morning and suffer the consequences of consuming fried chaat in the evenings. What were these young women trying to get at?

'We have been very agitated as it happened on our watch. We have now identified the culprit and want to conduct a trial today for deciding the punishment. We request you to preside over the proceedings.'

The newspaper slid out of his hand.

'Trial? Punishment?'

'You see, Pandit ji,' Varsha rushed on, 'You have always said that one must not conclude things without hearing all sides. While we are sure of our facts, we thought the right thing to do would be to hold a hearing to follow the principles of natural justice.'

Pandit ji took off his glasses and started polishing them.

'How soon can you be ready?'

'Anytime.'

'Request granted. We start after lunch.'

***

As soon as Varsha announced to the other members of the family that some sort of legal proceedings would take place in the afternoon, the excitement in the Haveli was palpable.

'Waah, Bhabhi! Did you actually ask Pandit ji to preside over the inquiry?' Madhu was candid in expressing her admiration.

'You should have heard her, Madhu. 'We want to follow the principles of natural justice'. I thought Pandit ji was going to have a fit.'

'Young ladies! Ladies! Here is some advice from veterans. Keep your points crisp, your body language confident and your notes handy.' The Awasthi brothers were doling out tips by the dozen.

'But who will act as the defendant's lawyer?' As four pairs of eyes turned to him, Vineet smiled. 'You hadn't thought of that, had you? I know you are determined to keep the name of the accused secret till the end. However, you must factor in his right to be defended too. You will need someone to speak for him.'

'Since it is Varsha Bhabhi on this side, let it be Randheer Bhaiyya on the other,' Madhu proposed.

Sudheer nodded in agreement, 'What an excellent suggestion. I second that.'

'Arrey! Will somebody let me decide, please?' Randheer laughingly interjected. 'It is against my chivalrous instincts to enter a contest in which there is a lady on the other side, especially when she stands no chance.'

'Don't underestimate, Bhabhi,' Vineet cautioned. 'And remember, she has the high ground. You do not even know the identity of the person you have to defend!'

'I agree, my irritating sibling and fan of Bhabhi. All those cups of sugar-free tea are making you speak this treacherous language,' Randheer was lofty in his dismissal. 'It's akin to fighting a duel with one hand tied behind my back. I'm up to the challenge. Even without any advance preparation, this will be an unequal battle. After all, my dear Watson, there is something called experience.'

Varsha bit back a sharp retort and mustered a fake smile for her husband. Inside her heart, she knew the game had changed inexorably. What had started in jest was now a battle for self-respect.

The warm pressure of Chhaya's hand on her arm was reassuring.

***

The grandfather clock sonorously chimed twice.

Pandit ji entered the drawing room that was rearranged to resemble a courtroom. He took his seat at the centre, with the mantelpiece providing a neat backdrop. Varsha and Chhaya were waiting on the left side. The rest of the family was on the right. Pandit ji was surprised to see that Indu had also joined them, pale and wan in an easy chair. The household staff including Chandra Prakash, Chedilal, Maharani, Gauri and Sundar stood behind them. In the middle, conspicuously vacant, was a stool for the accused.

With a formal nod of acknowledgement, he signaled that the proceedings should commence.

Varsha swallowed and took a deep breath. She started her argument.

'For the last few days, we have witnessed the strangest of thefts in this Haveli. Every morning, at exactly 9 o'clock, Pandit ji's breakfast was placed on the table. By 9:15, the time he took his seat, it would disappear. This happened for three consecutive days. It was then that Chhaya Bhabhi and I decided to do something about it. This morning, we set a trap to catch the thief.'

She paused here for dramatic effect. Every eye in the room was on her. The silence was punctuated by the rhythmic ticking of the timepiece.

Pandit ji observed that his daughter-in-law had skillfully captured the audience's attention. Everyone was waiting in breathless suspense. He nodded approvingly.

'I take the liberty to present the accused before this august court.'

Varsha paused again.

'Gauri!'

After a second of stunned silence, there were gasps and whispers all around.

'What?'

'It can't be…'

'This is not right, Mata ji. Stop her!'

After he recovered from his initial shock, Pandit ji rapped on the table with the wooden scale, borrowed from one of his grandchildren.

'The Court is brought to order. Order! Ms Varsha, this is a very grave allegation that you have leveled. I only hope you can back it with evidence.'

'Yes, Sir. I would like to invite witnesses for the purpose.'

'Fair enough. However, before we begin, we need a lawyer for the defence. Anyone?'

'I humbly offer my services,' Randheer stepped forward.

'Good. Will someone bring the young lady to the front?'

Until this point, Gauri had remained frozen with horror and shock. She was suddenly impelled into action. She fell at Indu's feet.

'Save me, Bhabhi. I'm innocent. I swear upon you. Save me, please.'

Indu looked tormented. This turn of events was unexpected.

As Chhaya half lifted Gauri, Indu laid a weak hand on Chhaya's arm and asked in a low tone, 'Are you sure, Badi Bhabhi?'

Chhaya nodded unwaveringly. A subdued Indu fell back with a whisper, 'At least, be gentle, Badi Bhabhi. She is only a young girl.'

Gauri was brought in front and seated on the stool. Randheer had occupied the seat next to her. Varsha rose and presented her witnesses.

'With your permission Sir, my first witness is Maharani.'

Maharani stepped forward looking hunted. She did not want any part of this.

'Maharani, you must swear to speak only the truth.'

'Bhabhi, if you don't trust me, why have you called me here. You know I've served this family for generations. I rue the day I joined this house.' With this, Maharani fixed a recriminatory eye on Mata ji.

There was the sound of suppressed laughter from the male quarters.

Seeing Varsha's fledgling legal career at risk of being nipped in the bud, Pandit ji intervened.

'It's all right, Maharani. You are an integral part of this household. And that is true for everyone who is present here. We trust each of you absolutely. Varsha is only following the process of the court. Let us humour her. But I promise you, including the accused here, that there will be no imprisonment. In fact, the harshest punishment that will be awarded is a day off.'

Laughter erupted but Pandit ji shook his head and continued somberly.

'I know, I know. Mata ji is protesting. But to my mind, the biggest penalty is to be identified as a failure, to be told you are not good enough and we do not want your services. Does that make everybody feel safer? Good. Should we start again?'

The mood lightened considerably with this proclamation. Gauri stopped sobbing and dabbed her eyes with her dupatta.

Chedilal and Maharani relaxed visibly. Only Varsha and Chhaya looked chagrined. But a warning glance from Pandit ji quelled their protest. He waved at Varsha to continue.

'Maharani, did you prepare breakfast today?'

'Of course, I did. You ate it, didn't you? What kind of a question is this?'

As Varsha looked stunned with this counter-questioning, there was an undeniable guffaw from Randheer, who quickly tried to masquerade it as a cough.

Pandit ji sighed in exasperation.

'Maharani, she is asking you a question. You have to reply in yes or no. Please do not ask her questions. Understood? Good. Can we hear your reply?'

'I did. I prepared breakfast for everyone.'

Grateful for Pandit ji's support, Varsha revived her questioning. 'What did you prepare for Pandit ji?' Maharani rolled her eyes, as if to say that she did not have time to waste. She opened her mouth to utter another angry retort when her glance fell on Pandit ji's severe face and she changed her mind.

'I prepared bread with butter.'

'How many slices of bread?'

'Four.'

'What did you do after that?'

'I kept them on the stone platform in the kitchen.'

'How many times did you prepare bread today?'

Varsha's question caught the audience and even the judge by surprise.

'Twice.'

'May this be noted, Sir. She prepared the bread twice today. Can you tell us why?'

'Well, the first time I did it like every day when Chandra Prakash told me. The second time you told me.'

Varsha nodded approvingly.

'Do you recall why I asked you to do so?'

Maharani's forehead furrowed as she tried to recollect the exact sequence. 'Let's see. Gauri had run into the kitchen blabbering something about missing toast and…'

Maharani clamped her hand over her half open mouth as realisation dawned on her. She looked aghast. All eyes turned to Gauri, She looked the picture of guilt, sitting with downcast eyes, staring at the floor.

'Thank you, Maharani.'

Pandit ji looked at Randheer, 'Any cross questions?'

'None, Sir.'

'You can go, Maharani. That was very good.'

Pandit ji's words of praise assuaged her feelings to some degree and a victorious Maharani returned to her place in the congregation. She received nods of approval from her fellow workers.

'My next witness is Mr Chandra Prakash.'

Chandra Prakash was as equanimous as always. He took his place unhesitatingly and swore to speak the unvarnished truth.

'Did you ask Maharani to prepare Pandit ji's breakfast today?'

'Yes, Ma'am.'

'At what time?'

'A little before 9.'

'What happened after that?'

'She placed the buttered bread on the kitchen platform. After that, you directed Gauri to take it to the dining hall. After a quarter of an hour, Gauri came running in. She looked frightened. She told us that the breakfast had disappeared. Chhaya Bhabhi had sent her to get another plate.'

'And what about yesterday and the day before? Did you get Maharani to prepare breakfast?'

'No, Ma'am,' Chandra Prakash neatly side-stepped the trap Varsha laid for him. By doing so, he proved himself to be a reliable witness. Pandit ji nodded approvingly at Varsha's slow but thorough style.

Chandra Prakash continued, 'I've been here yesterday and today, Ma'am.'

'Did you direct Maharani to get breakfast ready?'

'Yes, Ma'am. I was told on the first day that some hanky-panky had happened with Pandit ji's toast. He left for the court without eating anything for two days. I had strict instructions to make sure that he received his breakfast on time.'

'Did you follow those instructions?'

'Yes, Ma'am. Every day Maharani prepared the toast and Gauri took it to the dining hall.'

'Thank you, Chandra Prakash. That was most succinct.'

Pandit ji looked dumbfounded. He glanced at Mata ji and offered her a mute apology. Chandra Prakash's testimony exonerated her. He felt ashamed for having doubted her.

He cleared his throat loudly and said, 'Any cross questions?'

'With your permission, Sir,' Randheer rose. 'Chandra Prakash, was the breakfast handed over to anyone else?'

'No, Sir. In fact, today Chedilal offered to take it. But Varsha Bhabhi asked him to attend to the hot water. It was the girl who carried it.'

Varsha smiled triumphantly. Pandit ji made a note in his diary.

'Thank you, Chandra Prakash.'

'The next witness is Chedilal.'

While his colleagues were being questioned, Chedilal practised his lines. As a result, he described the morning's events, including the episode of the monkey, in less than a minute.

'Thank you, Chedilal. You have been most helpful. I would like to ask one more question,' Varsha said. 'What is it that the staff eat for breakfast every day?'

'Well, mostly Maharani makes parathas or rotis for us. We eat it with home-made mango pickle. Sometimes, if there is any bread left over, she gives it to Gauri. You see, she is the only one who likes bread. Maharani and I are old-fashioned and we prefer…', Chedilal's voice trailed off as the full import of his words hit him.

Gauri bowed her head in shame. The others vacillated between disbelief and embarrassment.

'That's all, Your Lordship.'

Pandit ji raised his eyebrows enquiringly at Randheer who quickly got to his feet for the cross-examination.

'When you heard the screams,' Randheer probed, 'did you rush out immediately?'

'Yes, Sir. Actually, I stopped for an instant to pick up a lathi. As you know, one can't battle monkeys empty-handed.'

'Did you notice whether the toast was on the table when you ran through the dining hall?'

'I did not pass through this room, Sir. I used the other exit to the garden through the court yard.'

'Are you saying that you did not go through the dining room at all?'

'No, Sir. I mean yes, Sir.'

'Did you see Gauri outside?'

'Not to begin with, Sir. Chhaya Bhabhi was running out and my entire attention was on her and Pinki. But later on, I saw Gauri.'

Pandit ji made some more notes.

'Is it possible that though Gauri was outside, you did not see her because you were focused on rescuing Pinki? That in fact Gauri was outside all the while but you did not notice her?'

Chedilal recognised an opening when he saw one. He grabbed the opportunity offered by Randheer.

'Absolutely, Sir. That is what must have happened.'

'I object, Your Honour. The Counsel is making suggestions to the witness and trying to put words in his mouth.'

'Objection sustained,' Pandit ji ruled with a frown. 'The Defence Counsel should stick to asking questions.'

Looking totally unrepentant, Randheer bowed mockingly to Varsha. With a respectful nod, Chedilal walked back. On the way, he patted Gauri reassuringly.

'The last witness is Ms Chhaya.'

Chhaya straightened her sari and stepped forward nervously.

'Ms Chhaya, where were you this morning between 8:30 and 9:30?'

'I was in the dining room.'

'What were you doing there?'

'I was supervising the children's breakfast. They came in around 8:30 and after having their breakfast, they ran out to play.' With every word, Chhaya's voice grew stronger and she felt more confident.

'Can you describe what happened after the children left?'

'Around 8:55, Gauri came in with Pandit ji's toasts. I told her to keep it at his place on the table and wait for him. I had seen him going to his room from the bathroom, so I knew he would arrive for breakfast anytime. I ordered Gauri to stand guard.'

'Point to be noted, Sir. Gauri was asked to stand guard. What happened after that?'

'We were both waiting. Suddenly, there was a piercing scream. You know the rest. When I came back, I saw the empty plate. At first, I thought Pandit ji had eaten his breakfast. Then I heard his footsteps and realised that the thief had struck once more. I got very scared. Mata ji would have killed us if we did not serve him breakfast today. Without further ado, I made Gauri run for fresh toast while I distracted Pandit ji.'

'You were not able to distract me, young lady,' Pandit ji sternly interjected. 'I decided to give you ladies another chance. Any cross questions?'

'Did you see Gauri take away the toast, Ms Chhaya?' Randheer was curt and slightly boorish, attempting to intimidate the witness.

'No,' it was a whisper.

'Then how did you conclude that she is the thief?'

'Objection, Sir,' Varsha was as quick as lightning. 'He is attempting to beat the witness into submission.'

'You need to improve your style, Randheer. This will not do,' Pandit ji's disappointment was evident.

Randheer fell back into his chair. Chhaya looked nervously at Pandit ji who nodded dismissively. She hurried back to her seat.

'With your permission I would now like to examine Gauri.'

Gauri felt the burden of each word. The utterances of the last three-quarters of an hour weighed heavily upon her. Her too-thin shoulders slumped. She looked like a criminal, bent over with remorse. Except Indu, at that moment, there was hardly a person in the room who would have vouched for her innocence. Including the Counsel for Defence.

'What are your duties in the morning, Gauri?'

Pandit ji nodded appreciatively. Varsha was trying to put the girl at ease; getting her to lower her defences. Circling around before moving in for the kill was a good strategy for beginners.

'I bring things from the kitchen to the dining room and also carry instructions back to the kitchen.'

'Do you run other errands around the house?'

The girl nodded mutely.

'What kind of errands?'

'Nothing specific,' Gauri shrugged despondently. 'Sometimes I fetch the newspaper for Vineet Bhaiyya, or play with Pinki, Guddu and Chikoo. I do whatever I'm told.'

Varsha felt the wave of sympathy swell around the room. She quickly changed track.

'This morning, did Badi Bhabhi tell you to watch over the breakfast?' Another nod of confirmation came from Gauri.

'Did you?'

'I was watching over it,' Gauri hiccupped. 'Suddenly Pinki screamed. I forgot everything and ran out.' A sob escaped.

'Are you saying that when you left, the toast was on the plate?'

'Yes, Bhabhi.'

'And when you returned?'

'It was gone.' This time Gauri could not control herself and began weeping.

'Was there anyone in the room when you left?'

'No, Bhabhi.'

'And when you came back?'

'No one.'

'That's all, Your Honour.'

Randheer was ready.

'Try and remember, Gauri. There must have been someone who came in as you were leaving.'

'I wish there were, Bhaiyya. I know you all think I am a thief. God alone knows that it is not so. But I will not lie. Not at all!'

Gauri's defiant words made many an eye moist. Even the wily Chedilal nodded sympathetically.

Pandit ji rapped on the table again.

'I presume that nothing more is to be said. Will both counsels present their closing arguments? Counsel for the Defence first.'

Randheer stood up and cleared his throat loudly. Pandit ji frowned. He disapproved of such theatrics.

'My Lord, this is a clear case of victimisation. She is an innocent, young girl, a juvenile who does not realise the full implication of her words. So much so that even when provided with a choice between maintaining her dignity and credibility and saving herself through falsehood, she has opted for the former. This speaks volumes about her personal integrity.

Moreover, there is not a shred of evidence against my client. No witness has seen her steal. There is no material evidence on record.

On the other hand, my client has a stellar reputation. She has no past criminal record and all the other witnesses have vouched for her honesty.

After considering all these circumstances, it will be a grave miscarriage of justice if she is punished for something that she has not done. I plead that she should be set free without imputing anything to her.'

As Randheer finished, Pandit ji gestured to Varsha. She collected her papers and stood up obediently.

'It is true my Lord that the accused is a juvenile. However, a crime, no matter how petty, is against the law and the innocent face of the accused cannot sway us. Let us be clear that we are here this afternoon to establish her role in this act or to clear her name.

It is true that I have not been able to bring forth any eyewitness. However, it is not necessary that there should be an eyewitness for every offence. If the courts started relying solely upon the testimony of a spectator, they would be put in a spot in many cases. Rather, I have built my case upon strong circumstantial evidence.

There are two aspects to any crime—motive and opportunity. The accused had a motive. She had over the years developed a liking for bread. She found it difficult to resist the warm, buttered toast.

The second is opportunity. Throughout the afternoon we have heard that there was no one in the dining room except the accused and Badi Bhabhi. The accused herself has admitted that when Badi Bhabhi left, the toast was intact.

I feel all sympathy for the accused. But *Themis*, the Goddess of Justice, cannot be emotional. I rest my case.'

A collective murmur went around the room. The case against Gauri was watertight. Randheer looked defeated.

'As we close the proceedings—'

'I want to speak too, Your Honour,' Guddu's high-pitched voice interrupted Pandit ji.

Pushing his moon-glasses down his nose, Pandit ji peered at his grandson. How many surprises were in store for him today?

'Yes, young man?'

'Actually, you are being very unfair. All of you are wrong in treating Gauri didi like a criminal. She is innocent.'

'And how did you decide this, Guddu? I thought I was playing the role of the judge.'

'Because I know who did it!'

An audible gasp emanated from the crowd. Many voices could be heard at once.

Pandit ji rapped his makeshift gavel.

'Do you wish to tell us who it is then?'

'I'll show it to you.'

Pandit ji shook his head in disbelief. Guddu had definitely inherited the theatrical skills of his grandfather.

'But for that I need some buttered toast. May I get some, please?'

In a few minutes the scene was set exactly as it was that morning—the toast on the plate. Guddu whistled. As the onlookers watched, Ruby bounded up to him. She looked questioningly at him and sniffed the air. Then she made a beeline for the table. In a jiffy, as smooth as silk, she lifted the toast clean off the plate and gulped it.

One could have heard a pin drop. Everyone seemed to hold their breath. Ruby's noisy slurping was clearly audible. She approached Guddu and rubbed herself affectionately against him.

'Oh Guddu! You are a darling. Thank you, thank you.'

Gauri flung her arms around Guddu. Maharani rushed to embrace them.

There was a lot of hugging and clapping. Relief was writ large on everyone's face.

Only Varsha felt deflated, a punctured balloon that has drifted down to earth. She started to leave.

'Wait!' Pandit ji's command stopped her in her tracks. She looked at him apprehensively.

'The matter is not over yet. We have been saved from a grave sin today. It is a lesson for this Haveli full of lawyers that an upright person must not be punished even if a thousand guilty ones escape. A ten-year-old boy has taught us this basic tenet. I salute him. He had the courage to stand up for a defenseless girl.

Yet, I must offer my felicitations to the two lawyers. Yes, Varsha. Do not look surprised. I am delighted with the way you argued the case today. Though I have not had the privilege of mentoring you, I hope you will agree to be my student. First, I suggest that you enroll for further studies in law.'

As Mata ji made a move to object, he continued firmly, 'As we have all seen today, your skills in the court will be more useful than in the kitchen. The sooner you realise that, the better it is.

Further, in order to atone for our deplorable behaviour today, we owe Gauri an apology. I hope you will find it in your generous and pure heart to forgive us, Gauri. You are a girl of strong character. I am proud to have you in my family. You are to revive your studies, if you wish.

And every morning, you are to be given buttered toast for breakfast.

The court is dismissed for the day.'

***

A PARROT, A MANGO AND A NECKLACE

Dawn had broken and bathed the cherry-hued Haveli in a dull, hazy glow. Wisps of mist, common at this time of the year in Aamnagri, clung to the bungalow like an over sized cloak. The first riser of the day, Gangu *mali*, was attending to his chores in the garden. Unbeknownst to him, he had company.

The Caucus of Foliage Dwellers or CFD had convened an emergency meeting in a corner of the sprawling campus of Pandit ji's Haveli. The venue was the usual spot—a shaded alcove formed by the roots of the ancient Bada the Banyan. Despite the early hour, most of the members of the CFD occupied their pre-assigned seats.

At the centre of the conclave, Monu the Monkey perched upon the gnarled hand-like formation of Bada the Banyan. He jumped up and down impatiently, eager to start the business for the day. The alcove was filled to capacity. Suddenly, Eki the Eagle flapped his huge wings, blowing a gust of wind into the otherwise sheltered nook. This was the signal everyone was awaiting. The proceedings commenced.

'Friends, Aamnagri citizens and my dear countrymen! Welcome to this extraordinary get-together.'

Monu's voice rose scratchily as he tried to catch the attention of the assembly. He had a penchant for drama and drew things out longer than necessary. The throng settled in for a long monologue.

'I am sure you are wondering why you have been summoned at daybreak when most of you should have been out to work. Because these are not usual times. Grave danger lurks in the neighbourhood. It needs to be tackled. This meeting is a clarion call for action. You might say ignorance is bliss. Why should I bother? Let me tell you why. Today if we sleep in our feathered nests and leafy boughs, our future generations will accuse us of criminal negligence.'

At the mention of nests and boughs, a murmur of protest emanated from the section where the birds huddled. After all, the blame for dereliction of duty ought to be shared by all members of the CFD. Picking on the avian members alone was unacceptable. Realising that he had committed a blunder, Monu quickly changed the subject.

'Friends, there is terrible news. Our reliable source, Totalal has sent us an urgent message.'

Another wave of whispering.

'What did you say?' Monu tried to guage his constituents' mood. 'Did I hear someone ask who is Totalal? You must be a newcomer, my dear, if you have not heard of Totalal. He is a privileged founder member of the CFD. At the same time, he enjoys a special status in the Haveli as Pandit ji's pet parrot. Since childhood, we have been taught to be deferential to his wisdom and acumen. A lot of weight is given to his words.'

'I don't know why this fellow repeats this at every meeting. Listening to him, one would think that we are getting new members by the dozen every day. Of course, everyone knows Totalal,' complained Peeli the Pigeon.

'You are absolutely right. In fact, the situation is the opposite,' concurred Chipu the Squirrel. 'In the last one month, half the birds have left, what with all the chaos here in the Haveli!'

'... have suffered immensely. You all know Pandit ji's grand daughter, Pinki is getting married in a fortnight. Relatives have been pouring into the Haveli for the past month. It has caused considerable inconvenience to the members of the CFD.' At this juncture, Monu's voice rose emotionally and became raucous: 'Bratty kids have chased us with sticks and slings. Callous workers have destroyed our homes. But we have grinned and borne it as our duty as members of Pandit ji's extended household.'

Monu paused for breath and then continued in a sharp voice. 'Let me remind you that generations of members of the CFD have sacrificed their health and happiness for Pandit ji's family. But now, things have come to a pass. The water is rising. We need to keep our heads above it.'

Again, he paused for effect, making sure he had gained everyone's unwavering attention.

Peeli the Pigeon looked around fearfully.

'I say, Chipu, where is the water that he is talking about? You know I'm hydrophobic. I don't want to be around if this place is going to be inundated.'

Chipu smacked his face with his palm.

'Peeli! He is saying that the situation is becoming dangerous. There is *no* water. Don't worry. It's just his verboseness.'

'May I have your attention, please? Or is your tête-à-tête of such great importance that it cannot be postponed?' Monu's brown eyes were fixed upon Chipu and Peeli.

'Uh-uh…'

Chipu resolved the matter by forcibly closing Peeli's beak and looking suitably contrite. Monu nodded in appreciation and turned to the others.

This interlude stopped other mumbled conversations and everyone was all ears. Satisfied that the audience was fully engaged, Monu dropped the bombshell.

'Friends, we have been informed that Sumeet is planning to cut the old mango tree in the inner courtyard. The space will be used to build the marriage mandap.'

Amidst gasps of shock and dismay, Monu's voice rose to a shrill crescendo.

'Yes, friends. Like you, I was shocked when Totalal shared this with me. Words failed our feathered friend as he relayed this piece of dreadful news. He choked with emotion. What? You say there must be some mistake? I wish there were. Alas! There is none. Totalal was a witness to the debate on this issue in the Haveli.

You ask what debate? Totalal said there was a war of words in the Haveli—between those opposing the cutting of the tree and Sumeet who vehemently championed it. Yes, there are *some* members in Pandit ji's household who are beholden to the mango, to the tree that has selflessly given them fruit and shade for decades. They battled for its life in Pandit ji's court. They argued, they cried, they pleaded.

The cold and rational prosecution counsel, on the other hand, stated that the tree is fruiting less with each passing year. I bow my head. The prosecution counsel stated that its branches are now weak and come tumbling down when the wind blows. I stand guilty as charged…'

'Monu is now warmed up. Get prepared for theatrics.'

'Shhh. Let's hear what he is saying. This is more serious than I presumed.'

'...but does it mean that I will not be given a chance to defend myself? No.

Does it imply that when I age and become frail, I will be discarded? No.

Those who cared for us and sacrificed their youth deserve our gratitude in the dusk of their lives. We need their blessings. The defence counsel has fittingly observed that cutting our brother, The Mango, right before an auspicious event in the family is not desirable.

However, friends, Goddess Themis is wearing a blindfold. She cannot see what is right. Despite these objections by some of the saner members of the family, frigid, selfish pragmatism won the day. They decided that it would be more economical to have the mandap in the inner courtyard. The hardheaded prosecution counsel added that wood from The Mango would come in handy for the puja and the havan during the marriage ceremony.

And now, prepare yourself for the final blow, my friends. Yesterday afternoon they finally decided to call in professional woodcutters. Totalal believes that the CFD must be told of this grave, impending danger as we have only twenty-four hours to save The Mango.'

A stunned silence followed Monu's impassioned speech. Then the members began to talk at the same time. For a few minutes, pandemonium reigned. Gangu *Mali* looked up from his weeding to see what was disturbing the birds and squirrels in the ancient banyan.

With a sardonic salute after his dramatic oration, Monu stepped down. Left leaderless, the creatures turned to each other in confusion. What should be done now? As if in answer to their unspoken question, Budha the Vulture jumped onto the perch that Monu had vacated. With his grey-white plumage and beady eyes, Budha automatically commanded respect. He was known to be sharp and decisive. The chattering ceased as the CFD members paused to hear their wise and venerated colleague.

'Brothers and Sisters, there is no time to be lost. Even as the sunrays darken the colour of the leaves and warm our wings and bones, a team of butchers will be on its way to strike at our refuge.

The Mango is our brother, planted long before any of us was born. For decades it has provided us food, shelter and comfort. You, your parents, your grandparents, indeed several generations, have enjoyed its hospitality. Babies have been warmly welcomed in its leafy limbs. And those like me, who are in the dusk of their lives, have dreamt of final peace in its frond-embellished abode. Are we to abandon it to the cruel axe wielded by greedy humans?'

'No! No!'

'Never! It will be a sin.'

'But what can be done?'

'We can't pretend to be helpless. Let's—'

A loud chant of no-no-no resounded in Bada the Banyan's hollow. Gangu Mali shook his head. Something wasn't right.

Budha the Vulture raised his left wing imperiously and those present became still.

'Yes. I agree with your "No". I say we cannot renounce our duty. We cannot abnegate our responsibility. If we do, we will never be forgiven by our successors.

In the past, whenever a crisis arose, we responded as one. My great great grandfather was the Commanding Officer of the first flock of this Haveli in the Battle of the Ravaging Bats. Today, I propose that some of us offer our services to form a 'flock' that will devise a plan to foil this terrible scheme.'

Budha's beady eyes were shining by the time he closed his yellow beak with a loud snap.

'But who will lead the flock?'

'Yes. We need a leader who is willing to sacrifice his life, if required.'

'Keeping with my family's tradition, if my brethren accept, I offer my services for this task,' Budha respectfully submitted.

At this, tremendous applause broke out. There was a great deal of clapping, chirping and cawing. Within minutes, the CFD notified a flock to prepare a strategy to outwit the humans. The subsequent events are a testimony of their courage and ingenuity.

***

In the verandah of Pandit ji's Haveli, the women were gathered for the customary analysis following and preceding any major function in the family. Chhaya sat surrounded by the others, basking in the glorious warmth of her peers' envy.

'Get me a glass of water, Gauri. My throat is parched.'

'As might be expected, Badi Bhabhi. You have been speaking without a pause.'

'Go away, naughty girl! Can't you see how excited I am? Everyone keeps asking me about last evening. Should I not tell them about the grand ceremony?'

'I just came in, Badi Bhabhi. I missed it all. Please fill me in. And you must start at the beginning.'

'Oh there you are, dearest Vinu! Anything for you. That you could come in spite of your commitments and the responsibilities at home! I only wish you could have made it earlier. Yes, yes, I understand. It is nothing short of a miracle that you are here at all. How is your mother-in-law now? I hope she recovers quickly. You do know that Vinod is a practising doctor, don't you? Once Pinki and he are married, you could consult him. Yes, yes, about the ceremony, as I was saying, when Mata ji and I went to Pinki's in-laws' place yesterday, we missed you terribly. Oh, what a house! My Pinki will reside in it like Queen Victoria.'

'I heard that they are a respected family of Benaras,' Rama Saxena remarked in a voice dripping with envy.

'Did you expect anything less for the granddaughter of Pandit Dinanath Awasthi? What a coincidence that Mr Shyamlal Pandey's father was Pandit ji's classmate. His wife was my mother's student many years ago. It's a small world.' Then with a wink, Chhaya gushed on, 'Not only are they a well-known family but they are also well-endowed. In fact, we took extra care about the gifts yesterday. After all, it should befit their standard, no? You can see for yourself today. They are coming in the evening for the devi puja to present new clothes and jewels to Pinki.'

Vinu joyfully hugged a blushing Pinki.

Chhaya continued, 'Ah! They have bought the finest silk from Benaras. Their family has patronised colonies of weavers for generations. It is they who are making the wedding clothes. Isn't it unlike anything we have heard of? And the ornaments! Only the purest of gold is being used. After all, she is their eldest bahu. Vinu, you *must* pay special attention to the gorgeous Ramtodi that Pinki's would-be-mother-in-law has brought for her. What a beautiful neck-piece, what workmanship! Their family has owned it for hundreds of years. Studded with diamonds, rubies and emeralds, I don't think anyone in our immediate or extended family has seen an ornament like it.'

Thereafter, Chhaya proceeded to describe the object in question in meticulous detail to the avid listeners.

'Wow! It sounds like a family heirloom. I can't wait to see it, Badi Bhabhi.'

'You will not have to wait too long. You see, they will present the Ramtodi to Pinki at the devi puja today,' Chhaya triumphantly announced to the breathless audience.

'You all are sitting here and chatting up. Come on. There is so much work to be done. After today's puja, preparations for the marriage will officially begin; invitation cards have to be sent out, the house has to be adorned with mango leaf garlands and marigold strings and the marriage has to be announced to the whole world.'

'Mata ji, Badi Bhabhi was telling us about the famous Ramtodi. I have attended many weddings, witnessed many devi pujas where the would-be-bride is presented with some jewellery. But none of us has ever heard of anything as magnificent as this. I can't wait to set my eyes upon it!'

'It is true. Pinki is a fortunate girl. All *Prabhu's kripa*!'

Chhaya had never felt so important in her life. She had seen the Ramtodi once at Pandey ji's house and knew its glitter would blind all the guests; the women would burn with jealousy. Rubbing her hands together in glee, she savoured the feeling.

***

The hour was declared auspicious and the priest blew the silver-encrusted conch shell. Vermillion and turmeric were pounded and ground, to usher in the joyous festivities; rose and marigold petals caressed the visitors' feet even as they were trod upon; incense sticks burned in silence while dispersing the sweetest of perfumes. The groom's family and guests arrived. Kanhaiya Lal Pandey and his wife Sunita warmly embraced Sumeet and Chhaya. Vinod sat down shyly in the mandap. The children laughed and showered petals on him. The devi puja began under the shade of the ill-fated mango tree.

At the appropriate time, Pinki was summoned. Sunita made a big show of taking out the Ramtodi from inside a suitcase. Every eye was fixed on the piece as it emerged, every neck craned to get a better view. Suddenly, there was commotion—a group of monkeys had entered the puja pandal and were shrieking and growling menacingly at the guests. There was a flurry of wings and a vulture swooped down, frightening people out of their wits. Totalal started screeching. Ruby began barking noisily. Havoc prevailed for a few seconds till Chedilal and Gangu Mali joined Sudheer and Vineet to restore order. Finally, the monkeys were chased away, Totalal was dispatched in his cage to the garden shed and the dog was locked inside the house. The guests heaved a sigh of relief.

'It was only the Lord sending us his blessings. After all, they have lived in this Haveli far longer than us and...' Chhaya made an attempt to inject some levity into the atmosphere. Before she could complete what she was saying, there was an anguished scream, this time from the groom's mother.

'The Ramtodi... It is missing!'

'What?'

'Where can it go? Look again.'

Chaos broke out once more as all the guests jostled with one another to search for the missing necklace. They rose and looked under their chairs; lifted plates and baskets filled with sweets and peered behind the gift boxes. All over the courtyard, there was a flurry of frantic movement. But to no avail. The Ramtodi had vanished into thin air.

A pall of gloom descended on the gathering. Pinki began sobbing softly. Chhaya sank into her chair like an exhausted athlete who has lost a strenous race.

Someone suggested calling the police, a suggestion that attracted censure all around.

'I'm sure, we will find it once the guests have departed. Let us not humiliate them by calling the police and questioning them.' Sumeet tried to calm down the others.

'But how will we complete the ceremony?' The groom's mother was understandably agitated.

'Don't be silly. A trinket cannot dictate our actions.' Kanhaiyya Lal reasoned. 'Let us start the puja. We have other gifts for the girl. Come on, Pandit ji. Let us not delay now.'

Thus, the devi puja was completed, albeit in a subdued and somber fashion, with a humble ring substituting for the magnificent Ramtodi.

***

It was late evening by the time the last guest departed. While the women began winding down the arrangements, the men went over the courtyard and the mandap with a fine-tooth comb. After a futile search, Pandit ji and Mata ji sat down in their high-ceilinged drawing room to discuss the alternatives before them.

'I don't see that we have too much choice in the matter,' Pandit ji was worried but he masked his anxiety and tried to speak in an equable manner. 'A priceless family heirloom has gone missing. I agree that we do not have any suspects or any clue as to how the theft took place. Nevertheless, it is a daylight robbery. Sooner or later, we *will* have to involve the police.'

'*Over my dead body*, Pandit ji,' Mata ji was equally adamant though not voicing her feelings as rationally. 'I shall not let you besmirch the family name. Calling the police in a home where a wedding is to take place! What will people say? The disrepute it would bring to us! All preparations for the marriage will be derailed. There is only one week left and so many chores have to be completed. If I listen to you, I'll spend the whole day answering the police's summons and before you realise it, they'll have my staff behind bars. No, I have thought of something else.

I have sent for Guru ji, the venerable saint from Bageechabad. I have absolute faith in him. He will be able to find the thief.'

'Listen to me, Shakuntala,' Pandit ji was insistent as he sensed the situation slipping out of his control. 'The police *must* be called while the scene of crime is still fresh. They might be able to find some clues.'

'No. I am *not* having the police in this Haveli, Pandit ji. I think I made that clear. I have always heeded your words. Yes, you might raise your eyebrows and look skeptical but I know how many times I have submitted to your directions against my better judgment. I am not going to relent on this occasion. There is too much at stake.'

'I distinctly recall that the last baba you invited into this Haveli was declared a swindler.' As Mata ji flushed in anger and embarrassment, Pandit ji pressed his advantage home. 'Do you know that the police arrested him a week after he visited us?'

As Mata ji turned accusatory eyes upon him, Pandit ji hastily clarified, 'No, no, I didn't have any role in his arrest.'

When Mata ji continued to stare at him disbelievingly, Pandit ji was forced to add, 'Okay, I did tip off the local police inspector when he met me in the court but that man had it coming. He was already on their list of wanted persons. He preyed on gullible women like you and spouted generalities that his victims wanted to hear. On that day, he knew about Chhote bhaiyya's accident because he spoke to the driver and servants before he came to see you. Shakuntala,' Pandit ji pleaded, 'please listen to me. This baba business will bring us nothing but disappointment.'

Even as they were arguing, Chedilal came in and announced that Guru ji had arrived. Mata ji immediately rushed out.

Guru ji was a renowned sage. His devotees swore by him. It was said that sensible rather than religious advice emanated from his saffron-robed demeanour. Not surprisingly, it struck a chord with his disciples and when adhered to, it produced remarkable results. Skeptics tended to deduce a direct co-relation between his level-headed advice, his followers' compliance and the desired outcomes. But such rational analysis cut no ice with his votaries. They believed he was endowed with mystical powers.

To be fair, Guru ji himself did not claim to have any special abilities. He acknowledged that the Almighty had bestowed the gifts of observation and intelligence upon him. He attributed all his success to *His* constant guidance and blessings, rather than his own greatness. He humbly accepted his critics' charge that what he said was common sense, rather than divination; only people obeyed it with greater fervour, believing that it was the Lord's will.

Thus, when Guru ji arrived at Pandit ji's mansion on that fateful evening, he was accompanied with a feeling of relief and hope. After a simple welcome, Guru ji immediately applied himself to the task at hand. To start with, he patiently heard the account of the disaster from Mata ji, from Chhaya and then from any other person from Pandit ji's family who volunteered to speak.

Thereafter, Guru ji granted an audience to the Haveli's staff in the confines of the courtyard. Their point of view was poles apart from their more educated masters. The helpers were convinced that paranormal agents were responsible for the inauspicious events of the day.

'I knew something was going to be wrong when the milk boiled over today,' Gauri told Guru ji while seeking confirmation from Maharani.

'I agree.' It was Ramu, the sweeper, hunched in a corner.

'Yesterday a mirror in the bathroom cracked. Today this happened. Pinki didi's wedding will only bring ill luck to this Haveli.'

'Even the animals have been behaving strangely all week—cawing and growling. The way they attacked the puja mandap today was extraordinary and unheard of. Some evil spirit has descended here.' Gangu Mali chipped in.

By the time this session ended, Guru ji was no wiser. Instead, with all the conversation about other worldly powers, a strange aura enveloped the house.

'Hai Ram! What was that?' Maharani clutched at Gauri's arm as a furry body slithered against her legs.

'Nothing, Didi. It's Ruby.'

'Maharani! Don't shout like that. You made me jump out of my skin,' Vinu reprimanded her.

'All this discussion of spectres is making me very nervous, Bhabhi,' Madhu whispered to Varsha.

'Me, too. Let's hope Guru ji finds a way out quickly. I don't like this. Aiee! Why do you have to creep up on me like this, Guddu?'

As they sat squirming, their hearts were heavy with dread. Every shadow seemed like a phantom and every creak was a call from the infernal regions. In this uneasy silence, with every eye in the household fixed on him, Guru ji sat in contemplation. To the onlookers, he appeared to be in deep thought.

'Do you think he has fallen asleep? His eyes are shut,' Guddu asked with the irreverence of youth.

'I think he is trying to make sense of the events by using his little grey cells a la Hercule Poirot,' Chikoo giggled.

'Shhh! Stop fooling around, you two.'

Oblivious to their observations, Guru ji concentrated on hearing his inner voice. His mind was speaking to him, it was telling him things that his eyes had seen without seeing, that his ears had heard without hearing. It was saying—

'*Don't cut the mango tree*'.

What??? Guru ji strained to hear his inner voice.

Instead, he heard Totalal, who had returned from his exile in the garden shed, chirping— 'Don't cut the mango tree'.

The bird then repeated it twice or thrice.

Guru ji opened his eyes and looked up, there was a giant mango tree overhead. Its huge canopy provided shade to most of the courtyard. In the dark winter evening, it was bathed in the warm glow of the moon. Through the trellis like branches, a few stars could be espied twinkling in the distance.

'What is the bird saying?'

'Nothing, Guru ji,' Mata ji brushed it off. She loved the old tree and was ashamed of their decision to chop it. 'That's what my grandson, Guddu, repeats the whole day and the parrot has picked it up.'

As Guru ji raised his eyebrows questioningly, Chhaya poured out the whole story.

'...the puja mandap for the wedding is to be made in the inner courtyard for which space is needed. Yesterday we decided to cut this old tree which has grown over the years to double its original size.'

As she spoke about their doubts and debates and then the final decision, Guru ji closed his eyes again.

Like an artist, he began sketching a pattern in his mind; like a scientist, he filled in the blanks; like an accountant he ticked off the numbers on the list.

First, the guests: The thought of the Ramtodi being stolen by one of them was preposterous; most of them were close relatives and well known to the family.

Next, the helpers: They were old retainers of Pandit ji whose integrity would not be compromised by a piece of jewellery, no matter how valuable. They had withstood far greater temptations.

Ruling out the bipeds as likely offendors, Guru ji turned his attention to the disturbing behaviour of the other inhabitants of the Haveli. There was the parrot, championing the mango's cause like a true-blood environmental crusader. Gangu Mali had observed discontent amongst the animals in the last few days. And the appearance of the monkeys and the vulture at the time of the crime seemed too much of a coincidence. Was it all connected or merely his imagination?

Guru ji was intrigued at the answer that his mind was suggesting; it was too fantastic, but then, the Lord's ways never ceased to amaze. Hmm. Guru ji scratched his head. It seemed to be the most likely solution to this riddle. But before speaking aloud, he wanted to seek His blessings.

'Mata ji, I see light at the end of the tunnel. But in order that we may dissipate the darkness completely, I need to perform a havan.'

Mata ji was delighted. She welcomed this diversion—anything that could draw their attention from this shameful incident at hand!

'Mata ji, while you make the necessary preparations, I would like to be left alone to meditate. I need to see the truth with my inner eye. However, I would like you to bring your pet parrot and leave him here.'

'Yes, Guru ji. Come on Chhaya, Indu, Vinu. Prepare for the puja immediately. Guddu, take Totalal to Guru ji.'

Once out of Guru ji's earshot, she muttered under her breath, 'I never wanted the mango tree to be cut. Inauspicious, I said. But nobody listened to me. Not Pandit ji, not Sumeet and definitely, not Chhaya. Now they have created this problem and I am expected to solve it. Thank God for Guru ji. His presence itself is reassuring and with him ordering that we organise a puja, I can feel hope awakening in my heart.'

'I always suspected him to be a fraud,' Pandit ji exhaled with disappointment but he made sure his voice was not loud enough to carry to Mata ji. 'Very soon, we will have the parrot pulling out the thief's name like road-side astrologers pull out one's horoscope.'

'Considering that we have no other alternative at this stage, Pandit ji,' Munshi Shyamlal commiserated, 'it is best to hold your tongue. Let us play along and watch. Who knows…'

As per Guru ji's orders, the courtyard was vacated and Totalal was brought before him, secure in his cage. Guru ji inspected the parrot carefully. It was a rose-ringed parakeet, a common bird in Aamnagri. The parrot reciprocated his scrutiny and fixed one beady orange eye on him. They spent a few minutes sizing each other up, like boxers in the ring. Guru ji thrust his face close to the caged bird.

He looked around to ensure that he was unobserved. After all he had a reputation to protect. Finding the coast clear, Guru ji whispered to Totalal, 'I'll save the tree. It's a promise. You ask your friends to leave the necklace on its branches tomorrow. Do you understand?'

Totalal looked at him unblinkingly and impassively.

For an instant Guru ji felt like a fool, striking a conversation with a parrot.

Then the bird gave the slightest of nods and turned away.

***

In less than an hour, Mata ji's team was ready for the second round of puja. Their bottled-up nervous energy of the last few hours bubbled out. They arranged fresh flowers at the altar, brought the ingredients for the havan and tripped over each other in their enthusiasm. On a signal from Guru ji, they all sat down, palms folded and heads bent in obeisance.

Guru ji began by loudly invoking the Lord. He sprinkled holy water at the altar and set the small pile of wood alight. He then scattered white flour, vermilion and turmeric forming intricate patterns that seemed to come alive in the light of the crackling fire. All the time, he chanted Sanskrit verses under his breath and offered oblations to *agni*. The heady smell of burning incense and the smoky ambience drugged the worshippers into a mild stupor. Suddenly he rose and walked away from the mandap. The surprised audience jerked awake and followed him with wide eyes. He stopped near the mango tree.

'O Holy Mango, accept my humble offerings to you.' Guru ji placed the bowl of fruit and flowers on the contorted roots of the tree.

'You have watched over this Haveli and its occupants for several generations. You have stood a witness to their rough times as well as their celebrations. Today, this family prostrates itself before you.' He turned towards Mata ji for confirmation.

She quickly bowed and the others followed suit.

'For a moment they had gone astray, they failed to think of all the times they received your protective shelter. On their behalf, accept my heartfelt apologies, O Wise One,' Guru ji poured some honey and milk on the roots.

Sumeet and Chhaya shifted uncomfortably while Mata ji's face glowed with triumph. Pandit ji was getting impatient, waiting for the mumbo-jumbo to end so that he could call the police. The household staff hunkered down in fear and discomfort; they could not understand what was happening. All they knew was that they were likely suspects and none wanted the police barging in. They fervently prayed for Guru ji's success.

Guru ji did not appear to notice the roller coaster of emotions roiling the gathering. He continued chanting mantras.

Suddenly he turned to the congregation, 'On behalf of these ignorant souls, I promise you, O Divine Mango, that none will harm you as long as this family lives here.'

Mata ji nodded vigorously.

But Guru ji was not satisfied. He wanted a commitment from the entire family. He swivelled around and fixed his coal-black, unblinking eyes on Pandit ji. Several minutes passed in silence. Pandit ji took out his handkerchief and wiped sweat from his brow. It was getting hot under his collar.

'Come on, Pandit ji. This is not the time to delay. You have to promise,' Mata ji nudged her better half.

'I promise,' Pandit ji wearily agreed. 'Anything to get this over and done with. If only I had my way, we wouldn't be wasting milk and honey—'

'Shhh! This is not the time to worry about these things. We need to concentrate with all our energy on what Guru ji is saying,' Mata ji zealously overrode his murmurs of protest.

'...are the nurturer, preserver and saviour. You are the hand of the Lord, opened in blessing over Pandit ji's family. They are *your* family. I pray to *Thee*, come to the aid of your family in this hour of need. They had strayed from the true path. Now they realise their error and are ready to make amends.'

As Guru ji continued with these exhortations and promises, unbeknownst to the humans, two members of the 'flock' were silently watching the proceedings from their perch above.

After an hour and countless promises, the havan ended. On Guru ji's directions, the day's activities were wound up and everyone retired. Only Guru ji continued to sit lost in deep thought with his eyes closed under the mango tree. Gradually, silence fell upon Pandit ji's Haveli.

In the stillness of the night, Chipu the squirrel, raced across to Totalal's cage. They twittered and chattered rapidly in the dark. Totalal relayed Guru ji's message to Chipu who scurried back to the flock.

Despite the late hour, Budha was pacing impatiently on the wizened branches of Bada the banyan as Chipu bounced in.

'O Leader! I have a message from Totalal,' Chipu exclaimed breathlessly.

When Budha heard Chipu's news, he cackled with delight. They had successfully saved their beloved friend, the old Mango. And now, that Pandit ji's family was repentant, it was time to be gracious.

'Good work, Chipu. Now listen carefully. Go and tell Totalal that we accept the offer. Tomorrow, the curtains will come down on this charade.'

***

The next morning, the household awoke early. Guru ji's orders were to assemble in the courtyard by 7:00 a.m. Pandit ji looked around at his drowsy grandchildren and shook his head. He had made up his mind to call the police if the necklace was not found by afternoon.

Guru ji took his seat at the promised hour and began with a short prayer.

'There are some of us who do not believe in the power of the universe,' Guru ji started with his gaze firmly fixed upon Pandit ji. 'To them I say, you are right in asking questions. We are all seekers. But sometimes, we get so engrossed in the quest that we do not realise when we attain our goal. Today, we must focus our minds and channelise our thoughts on the necklace.'

As the members of the household shifted in their Padmasanas and tried to open their mind's eye as directed by

Guru ji, Totalal shrieked, 'Don't cut the mango tree. Look in the mango tree.'

Guru ji's eyes flew open. He smiled.

'Mata ji, we can now safely walk on the path illuminated by the Almighty. Follow the bird's advice. Send someone to look in the old mango tree.'

Gangu Mali was hastily summoned and ordered to climb the tree.

Lo and behold! On the second branch to the left was the Ramtodi hanging innocently like a golden creeper glittering in the sun.

A collective cheer went up from the gathering. Guddu ran to feed Totalal some guavas. Chhaya and Pinki hugged each other and wiped tears of joy. Mata ji thanked the Lord and his agent, Guru ji, with bowed head and folded hands. The retainers wiped their brows; relieved, that after all, there would be no police investigation. Only Pandit ji stood nonplussed.

'Well, I never. Is it possible that a bird's testimony has solved this impossible looking case? How in the world?' Pandit ji shook his head in disbelief.

'That's all right, Pandit ji. As Guru ji pointed out, let us accept some things without endeavouring to discover the secrets behind them,' Chhote Bhaiyya consoled him.

'You are right. Above all, your sister has been proved right! Indeed, this day calls for celebrations.'

'Mata ji has thought of everything,' Vinu announced as she put an arm around her father. 'Even as we speak, Vinod's family is being informed of the recovery of their gift.'

'Undoubtedly the reporting is being done in a manner that, perhaps, alters the truth a wee bit.'

'How did you guess?' Vinu laughed. 'Not to mention that the amended version highlights the auspicious stars in Pinki's horoscope. But naturally, she will carry this good fortune with her to their home after the wedding.'

Amidst this festive turn of events, Chedilal approached the family cautiously, 'I know this is not the right time to ask this question, Pandit ji, but the tree-cutters have arrived. Should I...?'

The gathering burst out in loud guffaws.

As for the flock, it was another feather in their cap!

MATA JI'S QUIETUDE

'I miss the hustle-bustle of the old days, Gauri. Do you remember how we ran around like headless chickens in the mornings? There was always so much to be done and so little time!'

Gauri's smile mirrored the nostalgia in Chedilal's voice. She continued to roll out round chapatis for the dogs.

Chedilal shook his head as he rambled down memory lane. 'That one time when Indu Bhabhi had fever… I miss Sudhir Bhaiyya and his family. But above all I miss her. Every morning she was the first to get up along with us. Her smile…'

'I miss her too, Chedi Bhaiyya. However, we need to accept that things change and move on in life. In the Bhagvat Gita, Lord Krishna has—'

'Young lady, do not preach to me! You might sit with Mata ji for long hours, listening to her read the scriptures, but my hair has turned grey serving Pandit ji and his children. I have seen them grow up in front of these bleary eyes. Hmmph! Accept that things change,' Chedilal mimicked Gauri.

'Did I say that I do not want to accept change? No, but I find this disquiet unsettling. In all these years, I have not come across such silence, such…such… remoteness. As if a disaster is about to strike. Mark my words, something is amiss,' Chedilal wagged his finger in warning. 'Yes, something is definitely not right.'

'Stop it, Chedi Bhaiyya. I have heard your dire prophecies for years now. It is your overactive imagination. But you are right about the quietness, it is unprecedented. A stark contrast from the bustling Haveli I remember, where I came as a young girl, with our frenzied and manic lives, with no time to stop and ponder. I was raw, bumbling; with no clue about the way things were done. I shudder to imagine the trouble I must have caused Maharani in those days.

You can laugh as much as you like, Chedi bhaiyya but I was a handful. Yes, a real pain for Maharani. When she finally left the Haveli to go to her village two years ago, she confessed that she had not wanted to keep me at the beginning. Too much of sass, she said. Mata ji overruled her. Over the years, we learnt to work together and developed a fondness for each other. When we bade her farewell, I could not stop crying. I felt I was losing my best friend.'

There was a moment of silence as both gathered their thoughts.

Then Chedilal asked, 'What are you implying, Gauri?'

'Something that *you* refuse to yield to, Chedi Bhaiyya: time changes everything. The tiny children who rode on your shoulders are grown men and women, bringing up kids of their own. They are hardly recognisable. Neither are you for that matter. Look at you, your moustache has grayed along with your hair.'

'At least I have not put on weight, young lady. You seem to be intent upon following in Maharani's footsteps in all respects, including her girth.'

Gauri chortled.

'Age has not dampened your sense of humour, Chedi Bhaiyya. I know, I'm becoming stout. It is all this young Lakshmi's doing,' Gauri playfully caught hold of a dark-eyed teenager standing beside her and hanging on to every word.

'Ever since this girl has come, I hardly move around. Life has come full circle—I am in Maharani's shoes and Lakshmi is my tormentor.'

'Any news of Indu Bhabhi?'

Gauri shook her head sadly.

'I haven't heard anything from Mata ji. Ever since Sudheer Bhaiyya shifted his family to Dharampur, they rarely visit Aamnagri. Too far away, I suppose. A Haveli that seemed so tiny once has spare space that lies unused today. Come to think of it, we have not opened some of the rooms for years. You should be grateful for it, Lakshmi. In those days I would run from one end of the Haveli to the other to attend to errands. Maharani couldn't sleep at night because I would cry that my feet hurt.'

'You are right, Gauri. In fact,' Chedilal dropped his voice conspiratorially, 'last night I heard Mata ji lamenting that the children had not come home for two years. Not even to celebrate the festivals together.'

'Is that so? Let me see, Chhaya Bhabhi and Varsha Bhabhi were here on Diwali when Maharani was making *gujiyas*. Oh my god! It's been two years. Isn't that surprising?'

'Not if you ask me,' Chedilal was philosophical. 'If you pull at something too hard and for too long, it is bound to snap. Mata ji tried to impose her will upon her children; more than they could tolerate. One by one, the birds flew from the nest.'

'I guess you are right. The first break is the most difficult to give in to. After that, it is only a matter of time before the rest crumbles. I remember Mata ji was extremely upset when Sudheer Bhaiyya proposed the shift to Dharampur. He was always the one to take the bull by the horns, our Sudheer Bhaiyya. He never shied away from doing what he thought was right.'

Chedilal nodded in agreement. 'We all know that Indu Bhabhi was the chain that linked the members of this household together. Her goodness bound them. But how long could she be expected to sacrifice her happiness and stay alone while Bhaiyya was posted outside. I think Sudheer Bhaiyya did the right thing. As soon as he got family quarters, he shifted them to Dharampur. Is it true that the schools there are quite fancy?'

'That they are. When Chikoo came on Holi three summers ago, she had the airs of an accomplished lady. Indu Bhabhi said she was attending dance and music classes and was even learning to paint.'

'Their shifting from Aamnagri was justified. But I really do not approve of the other three moving out of their father's Haveli. As if he could not feed them or their families.'

'You said it at the beginning, Chedi Bhaiyya. The birds stretched their wings. They cannot be kept caged by force anymore.'

'I know, I know. That does not mean I support it,' Chedilal concluded waspishly. 'At any rate, enough gossip for the day, young woman. Don't you have work to do? And you, Lakshmi, are you planning to stand here the whole day or will you get the water boiling? It's time for Pandit ji's bath and you haven't even started the fire. Hurry up!'

Lakshmi stuck out her tongue at Chedilal's back.

The more the surroundings changed, the more they remained the same.

***

Things had indeed changed in Pandit ji's Haveli. About five years ago, one by one, his sons set up house independently, leaving Bangla Number Unnees as woebegone as the day the family stepped into it.

Sudheer relocated his family to Dharampur where he was posted in the Army cantonment. Randheer and Sumeet shifted to separate homes in Aamnagri though they continued to work with Pandit ji. Varsha completed her legal studies and joined them. Vineet and Madhu moved to the capital city of Indraprasth where Vineet took up the job of a tax lawyer of a leading multinational company. Madhu taught in a neighbourhood school.

Summer continued to visit the Haveli every year, parijat trees scattered their blooms in the fragrant breeze, mangoes beckoned parrots and koels, but the Haveli remained stubbornly reticent to their overtures. There were no visitors. The demon of work had enslaved its occupants and drawn them away from the simpler pleasures of life.

'Lakshmi, have you fed the dogs?' with age, Mata ji's voice had lost its high pitch but not its intensity. Neither had her affection for the dogs abated. The older Ruby and Blackie had departed to frolic in the blue skies above. It was their progeny who continued to toil as loyal soldiers in Pandit ji's Haveli. She patted Snowie, the youngest dog affectionately. With no one awaiting her arrival back home, the duration of her morning visits to the temple became longer.

'Get me a cup of tea. Has Pandit ji eaten his breakfast? No? Good. Then bring my tea to the dining room. I'll have it with him.'

As she fitted her petite frame into the ornately carved, heavy dining chair, Mata ji recalled her conversation with Vinu that morning. She had invited Vinu to come with her family and spend a few days at the Haveli.

'Mata ji, you know how it is! Sonu changed his job last month. He shall find it difficult to get leave. Monu is busy preparing for his MBA exams.'

'You make the children work too hard, Vinu. You should give them some time to relax,' Mata ji attempted to build up a case for a vacation in Aamnagri. 'What is this? Constantly chasing some goal or the other. It's not—'

'Well, if you've called to lecture me on my parenting skills, then you have chosen the wrong day. I asked the boys about a trip to Aamnagri. They refused. And since you find me to be lacking in every respect, there is no point in my coming over alone.'

With these words, Vinodini slammed the phone down.

Mata ji felt like her daughter had slammed a door on her face. No matter how hard she tried, she could not get in. For a long time, she stared blankly at the receiver buzzing in her hand. Then with utmost care, she placed it back into its cradle.

'I'm sorry, Darling,' she whispered tearfully. 'You were always my favourite child. How could I consider you a poor parent? It is I who failed. I called to hear your voice, not to have an argument that ended on this bitter note.'

She hung her head in shame. The previous day she had similarly tried to get Anu and Sumi to agree to come to Aamnagri during the summer break. Their responses were identical albeit more even-tempered.

'Mata ji, the children are no longer in school with summer breaks when the whole family can travel. Now they are working in different places. It is not easy for them to take leave.

Me? Of course, I would love to come to see you and Pandit ji. But you know how it is… The maid is new. In my absence, she will not lift a finger. It becomes extremely difficult for others if I am not around. Why don't we plan something after Diwali?'

Four summers and three Diwalis passed with Mata ji trying to find a slot in her children's calendar. It was unbearable for her. All her life, she drew sustenance from the love and affection of her family. She could not fathom what had gone wrong that they no longer wanted to be with her.

'Why are you frowning so early in the morning, Mata ji? I hope it isn't something that Munshi's done,' Pandit ji joked as he took his seat at the head of the table.

Mata ji smiled feebly and shouted for Lakshmi to bring breakfast. She was overcome with a desire to weep. To hide her face, she started polishing the worn-out sun mica tabletop with the end of her sari.

Pandit ji recognised the tell-tale signs of disquiet but knew better than to ask.

As they waited awkwardly, Pandit ji opened the morning newspaper and started scanning the headlines.

'Are Randheer and Sumeet coming to the court nowadays, Pandit ji?'

Silence.

'Pandit ji? Did you hear me?'

'I did.'

'And?'

With a deep sigh, revealing his long-drawn suffering, Pandit ji neatly folded and put away his newspaper. He pushed his moon-shaped spectacles down his nose. In the past, they had a grave impact on the person in front. Now they were bent and they made him look like a shriveled owl instead.

'You ask me this question *everyday,* Mata ji. For heaven's sake, you can't be expecting a different reply!'

Mata ji had the decency to look embarrassed.

'If you are missing your sons, why don't you call them?'

Mata ji shook her head vehemently.

'Never! They walked out of this Haveli ignoring my tearful pleas. They don't know what they are doing. They are under their wives' spell.'

'Ha! That's what every mother thinks. I'm sure, my mother thought the same of you. No, no.' Pandit ji backtracked hastily as he saw Mata ji's visage darkening, 'Not about you, of course. I meant it in a more general sense, and uhh- uhh, about Veena and Rita Bhabhi. You were a model bahu,' he improvised wildly.

Mata ji's expression showed she was unconvinced, so he quickly continued, 'In reply to your question, Randheer and Sumeet are both fine. So is Varsha. She argued brilliantly in Justice Kumar's Court yesterday. All the lawyers came over and congratulated me. You cannot imagine how proud I felt. After all, I have tutored her.'

'Let me know when you are through waxing eloquent about your daughter-in-law. I have something to discuss.'

Any discussion with Mata ji entailed a monologue in which Pandit ji's contribution was limited to emitting soothing noises conveying agreement. He might as well get it over and done with right away. So he nodded encouragingly as he bit into his toast.

'Of course. Tell me what's preying on your mind.'

'Well, for some days I have been thinking about the past. We were a happy family, living together under the same roof. But someone has cast an evil eye.'

Pandit ji suppressed a groan. Was Mata ji going to start dabbling with witch hunters and astrologers again? He hoped not.

'As I was saying, it's been a long time since we were together. Why don't we organise a family reunion? Have the children, grandchildren, everyone come over.'

'Ah!' Pandit ji sighed audibly. 'That is an excellent idea. Though infinitely more expensive than the babas that you bring, it is a far more palatable proposition.'

'What Baba are you talking about? Did I mention any? If it is the Baba who came to bless Chhote Bhaiyya—'

'No, no. Forget it. It was a slip of tongue. I was merely admiring your vision. It's a wonderful plan. When do you want to have this, eh, reunion?'

'The summer break would be perfect. There will be two weeks of vacation in Court. Hopefully, the others can spare some time.'

'I have no objection. Why don't you ask them?'

'I, um, did,' Pandit ji stared incredulously as a stammering Mata ji narrated the morning's ordeal.

'What should we do?' Mata ji's plaintive cry would have melted the hardest of hearts.

'Let us try with Indu and Sudheer first. And then Randheer and Sumeet. Once a few of them agree, the others can be roped in with ease.'

Mata ji brightened considerably.

'You are right. I shall ask Indu. She will not refuse me.'

Having fulfilled his duty, Pandit ji went back to his newspaper. Mata ji remained in deep thought with her brow furrowed.

Pandit ji stole a glance at her. In all likelihood, she was planning her conversation with her deferential bahu. Best of luck, Indu!

He smiled. For once, Mata ji's suggestion was flawless. A reunion! It would be good to have the family in the Haveli. He missed the laughter and the bickering.

Pandit ji pulled himself up and cleared his throat. He was *not* an emotional old fool.

***

Despite Pandit ji's determination to avoid sentimentality, he found his thoughts straying during the day.

'What happened, Pandit ji? Your mind is elsewhere,' the astute Munshi noted.

'Huh? Nothing. But I think I will go home early today.'

By the time Pandit ji returned home, the parijat trees in the drive way cast misshapen shadows in the evening darkness. Cicadas chirped and the wind rustled the leaves, bidding good bye. Another day in their life had drawn to a close. Shaking off a sense of unease, he made his way towards Mata ji; a solitary figure morosely pacing the lawn. She had always been petite but her body seemed to be carrying a load heavier than usual. He felt a twinge of disappointment, unbidden and fleeting… This will not do, he ordered himself sternly. So he masked his mood behind a cheerful veneer and injected gaiety in his voice as he called out to her.

'Good to see you take the doctor's advice of regular exercise. How many rounds have you done?'

'I didn't count,' Mata ji was melancholic.

Snowie bounded up to greet Pandit ji with a loving lick.

'My little girl! Did they give you something to eat? No?'

'Are we doomed to pet these four-legged beings for the rest of our lives, Pandit ji?' Mata ji was woebegone. 'I spoke to all our children today. No one has time to come over to see us. Even Indu! Exams, jobs, tuitions. Their life is reduced to targets, ticking off items in a wish list. They do not realise that this moment, once gone, will never return. While they are busy toiling for the future, their present is passing by unnoticed.'

Pandit ji had no response. He continued scratching Snowie behind the ears.

The silence stretched on interminably.

At last, Mata ji let out a deep sigh and with slumped shoulders, walked away.

***

'Chedi Bhaiyya, have you seen Mata ji? It is long past her lunch hour.'

'No, Gauri. I saw her when I gave the lunch box to Sundar. She was in the drawing room looking at the photos displayed on the wall. I haven't seen her after that.'

'Lakshmi, check if Mata ji is in her room. Ask her if she would like to have her lunch now. Do not disturb her if she is asleep. This is very unusual. Mata ji is quite particular about her lunchtime.'

Within a few minutes, Lakshmi was back. Mata ji was not in her room.

'Where could she have gone? Did she say anything to you?'

Lakshmi shook her head. Perplexed, Gauri and Chedilal looked at each other.

'Perhaps she has gone to visit Mrs Tiwari or one of the houses nearby,' Lakshmi volunteered.

'Not Mata ji. She has not gone calling upon neighbours for as long as I can remember. I wonder where she might be…'

***

It was late in the evening and there was no sign of Mata ji. When Pandit ji returned from the court, he found a worried-looking Gauri and Chedilal waiting on the porch.

'Thank God you are back, Pandit ji. We have been waiting for you for the longest time…'

On any other day, Pandit ji would have allowed Gauri to babble on, circumambulating the issue and taking her time to come to the crux of the matter. But her tearful countenance rang an alarm bell in his mind.

He cut her off midway, 'What happened, Gauri?'

'It is Mata ji…she is missing…since morning.'

Pandit ji smiled. The situation was not as grave as Gauri thought. He was aware of his wife's penchant for taking off without any notice. Generally, it meant a visit to her brother's house in Bageechabad.

'Chedilal, have you checked with Chhote Bhaiyya?'

Chedilal nodded.

'And?'

'Mata ji has not gone to Bageechabad, Pandit ji. Rather, Chhote Bhaiyya became very worried and asked me to inform you immediately.'

'Well, then why didn't you?'

'I called up Munshiji. But you had left for Justice Kamat's chambers.'

'It is all right,' Pandit ji nodded with mild irritation. 'Go and check with the neigbours. Mata ji is not a child to have lost her way. She must be *somewhere*.'

***

The grandfather clock chimed eight times. The Haveli was in darkness. A semi-circular pool of light spilled out through the open door of the drawing room. Gauri came into the dining room and switched on the bulb. A shadowy figure slithered along the wall and she almost jumped out of her skin.

'Aieeee…'

'What happened, Gauri? Why are you shouting?'

'I saw her, Pandit ji,' Gauri was wild-eyed and hysterical.

'What nonsense! You have been watching too many silly films that put ridiculous ideas into your head.' 'No, Pandit ji,' Gauri was vehement. 'I swear. It was Mata ji. She went out. Towards the lawn.'

'There is only one way to find out. Follow me.'

Pandit ji strode outside determinedly. He flicked on the switches so that the driveway was bathed in the yellow glow of incandescent bulbs.

Empty.

'See, there is no one here.'

Gauri peered obstinately at the desolate path, seeking a trace of a shadow.

After a few seconds, she sighed deeply, 'I'm sorry, Pandit ji. But I am sick with worry. I hope, Mata ji is all right.'

'Of course she is, you foolish girl. Now run along and get my dinner. I am starving.'

Despite his outwardly genial demeanour, Pandit ji was unable to swallow more than a few morsels of food. In his mind, he was replaying his conversation with Shakuntala that morning—her craving for the children and his indifference to her anguish.

'If only I had paid more attention to her. Perhaps I could have assessed her state of mind. If she was perturbed, I could have counseled her…unlike her to leave in this manner. Even

Chhote Bhaiyya is unaware of her whereabouts… Where have you gone, Shakuntala?'

Chedilal found Pandit ji in this state, muttering and berating himself on his return. In the last few hours, Chedilal had visited all the neighbours and acquaintances to enquire about Mata ji. On seeing him, Pandit ji's eyes lit up.

'Any news?'

Chedilal's downcast eyes and crestfallen appearance gave him the answer.

Pandit ji closed his eyes briefly and made a concerted effort to sound confident.

'I am sure we will have some news tomorrow. You eat dinner and lock up the house.'

That night, Pandit ji understood what it felt to sleep on a bed of thorns. The smooth, cotton bed sheet felt abrasive, prickling his skin; the whirring fan grated on his nerves and the chatter of the cicadas annoyed him. When he woke up in the morning, he was in a foul mood, sapped of energy and disgruntled with the turn of events.

'Shakuntala has a sense of perfect timing. To vanish when I have the most important engagements lined up is highly irresponsible. Always seeking attention! That is her problem. I wonder where she has disappeared.

Tiwari's wife was my best lead but Chedilal says she has no clue. Tiwari, poor chap, called last night to sympathise with me. He confirmed that his wife was innocent, at least in this instance. Now where am I supposed to go looking for her?' Pandit ji shook his head wearily. 'Let me call Chhote Bhaiyya. He knows Shakuntala in and out. He would have some idea.'

Relieved at the thought of having a plan in hand, Pandit ji rushed through his customary routine and dialled Chhote Bhaiyya shortly after breakfast. Unfortunately, Chhote Bhaiyya was out, inspecting his mango orchards.

'What happened, Pandit ji? You sound disturbed,' Malati, Chhote Bhaiyya's wife, asked in a voice filled with concern.

'Nothing. It's nothing. When is he returning?'

'He said he would be back by late evening. I shall ask him to call you. Are you sure everything is all right? Where is Didi? Chedilal was asking about her yesterday. Has she returned?'

Pandit ji was at a loss for words. With no satisfactory rejoinder at hand, he brusquely changed the subject. 'I have to rush to work now. Do tell Chhote Bhaiyya to call me as soon as he returns.'

For a long time, Pandit ji stared at the black telephone in his hand.

'This instrument caused terrible misery to Shakuntala yesterday. Could she have… No, no. Shakuntala is made of sterner stuff. But the children's behaviour had upset her… Could she have…'

At that moment Pandit ji spotted Chedilal hovering near him like an uneasy mother hen. His irritation increased.

'Can't I have any peace in this house? Why are you lurking in the corners, Chedilal?' he grumbled.

But Chedilal was a stalwart and not one to be put down by harsh words.

'Why don't we inform Sudheer Bhaiyya and the others, Pandit ji? They are as responsible for Mata ji's well being as you. Or should we ask the police to search for her?'

'Please keep your wisdom to yourself, Chedilal,' Pandit ji replied testily. 'Do you think I am an imbecile? Of course, I shall be speaking to Randhir and Sumeet when I meet them in the court.'

'And the police?'

'What about the police? I presume you have not understood Mata ji at all if you are suggesting that we should send the police after her! She shall skin you alive once she returns.' The last managed to bring a hesitant smile to Chedilal's wisened face. He bowed meekly.

'Whatever you say, Pandit ji.'

***

The day passed slowly. Achingly so. Pandit ji broke the news of Mata ji's disappearance to his sons in the court who immediately conveyed it to their siblings. For the next two hours, Pandit ji was left fielding phone calls from his daughters, daughters-in-law and older grandchildren. Unaccustomed to handling such a high volume of conversation, Pandit ji felt incapacitated and depleted by lunch time.

'Munshi, I don't think I can carry on.'

'Why? What happened, Pandit ji?' the usually unflappable Munshi allowed the slightest trace of concern to creep into his voice.

'I did not get proper sleep last night. The heat was enervating. I feel thoroughly exhausted. The sciatica in my leg is also acting up. I'm going home. You carry on here. And bring the case files to Haveli in the evening.'

Munshi watched with sympathy as Pandit ji hobbled out to the waiting car.

'Poor man! At his age, to have everything and yet nothing… Without Mata ji he will be unbearably lonely.'

Munshi opened his folding desk and sneaked a peek at the dog-eared picture of Lord Hanuman that he kept hidden inside.

'O *Sankatmochan*! You alone can relieve Pandit ji of his woes. Let Mata ji be safe.'

***

Seven days later, the situation had not improved.

'I can't believe it, Chedi Bhaiyya. A week has gone by and still no news of Mata ji. The police have sent out look-out notices for her in all the nearby places. But there is no sign of her. Her friends have not heard from her. I've been thinking so much about her that I couldn't sleep last night. Today morning, the first thing I did is call Guru ji's *mutt*. She hasn't gone there either. Has the earth swallowed her?'

'I am also worried, Gauri. Have you seen how haggard Pandit ji looks? He is barely eating anything to keep his body and soul together.'

Gauri wiped away a stray tear.

'I know. Thank God, Vinu didi has come. Pandit ji could never say no to her. She is trying her best to cheer him up and get him to eat his meals.'

'But who will take care of her, Gauri? I found her sobbing in her old room last evening. She was ruing the conversation she had with Mata ji that day. Apparently, they had quite a showdown. Harsh words were exchanged. Poor didi! She thinks this is all her doing…'

'I heard Badi Bhabhi say that Sumi and Anu didi will reach today. Isn't it ironic,' Gauri's eyes misted, 'that it is like the old times, with everyone congregating in the Haveli. But the centre of the universe is absent.'

'I know what you mean. Though he made a show of protesting, Pandit ji was secretly relieved to have Randheer and Sumeet Bhaiyya come over with their families. You should have seen the way he went about getting the rooms aired so that they could be comfortable. For a few hours, he was like the Pandit ji of old. And then the shadow returned, Gauri. The dark shadow that I have seen on his face so many times this last week.'

'Chhote Mama and Mami's outburst last week has not helped matters either. Chedi Bhaiyya, we all knew that Malati mami never liked Mata ji. Therefore, I was shocked to see her blaming Pandit ji for this mess. Chhote Mama was inconsolable and hardly spoke a word. But his reticence, while Mami made wild accusations, must have cut deeper than words.'

'Pardon my saying so, Gauri, but Chhote Bhaiyya was always an insipid ninny. Love for his sister has blinded him. He respects Pandit ji enormously but lacks the courage to check his wife. Malati does not realise that the man she is abusing is responsible for her happiness. Without Pandit ji's backing, Chhote Bhaiyya would have become bankrupt.'

'Yet, not all of what Mami said was false. It is true that Mata ji was feeling abandoned. Pandit ji hardly spared any time for her. And the children, the lesser we speak of them the better.'

'What do you mean? Should Pandit ji stop doing everything and sit at home to hold Mata ji's hand the whole day?' Chedilal bristled with anger at this slight to his master.

'Now, now, Chedi Bhaiyya. Taking umbrage will help no one,' Gauri spoke soothingly. 'Pandit ji has enough to fend for himself and Mata ji. The children are self-sufficient. Don't you think a little consideration to Mata ji might have helped?' Gauri continued with feminine insight, 'The way he is missing her now, I wish he had let her know that she was wanted when she was around. She felt rejected and unloved. She was never a popular person. Her family was her mainstay. To have them desert her was the ultimate punishment.'

'But—'

'I know what you are going to say. One does not walk out of the house despite one's problems,' Gauri sighed. 'You may be right. But who knows what was going on in Mata ji's mind. Perhaps she felt that life, as it was, was not worth living.'

'Stop it, Gauri! You have become like Maharani, making wretched pronouncements. I am sure, Mata ji is fine.'

'I hope—'

'Arrey, Indu Bhabhi! When did you arrive? Here, give me your bag.'

'Wonderful to see you again, Indu Bhabhi,' Gauri touched Indu's feet and was drawn into a warm embrace. As the two women held each other, unbidden tears flowed down their faces. Wiping away the tell-tale signs quickly, Gauri rushed headlong into work.

'Let me make a cup of tea for you while you bring me up to speed about everything that has happened. With you in the kitchen, it feels like the good old times are back, doesn't it?'

***

In the afternoon, Pandit ji sat down in the drawing room, surrounded by the members of his family. There were his four sons, their wives, and three daughters with their spouses and a few grandchildren who had managed to make it to Aamnagri. Gauri, Lakshmi and Chedilal lurked in the shadows of the dining hall, hanging on to every word.

The fan whirred as they noiselessly grappled with wayward, unpleasant thoughts.

Finally, Sudheer spoke, 'It has been ten days. There is no news of Mata ji. The SP called me last evening. He said that he is not optimistic about finding her. How long are we going to mope and wait for bad news to arrive?'

'You are right, Bhaiyya. Yet how can Mata ji vanish into thin air?'

'We are all stunned, Vinu. But after failing to trace her for ten days, we must accept reality.'

There was an uncomfortable pause. They knew what had to be done. They lacked the courage to voice it.

Eventually, Indu walked over to Pandit ji and placed a caring hand on his slumped shoulders.

'Pandit ji, I know this is very painful for you. If I claim to understand your suffering I would be lying. Your grief is yours alone. We cannot share it or lessen it inspite of our best intentions. I have no cure for it. What I do know is that prolonging it would bring you greater sorrow.

What we cannot change, we must accept. Even though it is agonising. I feel foolish preaching to you who have seen more than I could begin to imagine. But sometimes we need to be told certain things. The facts are staring at us in the face, Pandit ji. Though it goes against our wishes or our readiness, we have to accept reality. Mata ji is gone.'

Here, Indu's voice choked and her body shook. She seemed incapable of carrying on further. Vinu came and put an arm around her.

Taking a deep, calming breath, Indu summoned up the last vestige of fortitude and tried to infuse some of it into the solitary figure.

'Pandit ji, you are the head of this family, the master of this Haveli. We look up to you for guidance. In these trying times, if you fall apart, what will become of us? Please, Pandit ji. For all our sakes, you must pull yourself together.'

'Bhabhi is right, Pandit ji,' Vinu lent support to Indu. 'We have lost our mother. We cannot afford to lose our father.'

One by one, the rest walked up to Pandit ji's chair and surrounded him. Some clutched his cold hands; others sat near his feet with their heads on his lap. A heaviness hung in the air, born of unshed tears and choked emotions.

Gauri and Chedilal were crying unrestrainedly in the adjacent room. After a few moments of poignant silence, Pandit ji spoke up. He made a herculean effort to sound cheerful.

'Well, children, you have left an old man with no choice. Mata ji would never forgive me if she thought I was shirking my responsibility towards you.'

There were relieved smiles all around. In that moment, the heavy blanket of depression weighing upon them evaporated into a fine mist of tears and sighs.

'Pandit ji, you are a rogue…'

'God bless your sense of humour, Pandit ji.'

'I can almost imagine Mata ji chastising you!'

Pandit ji grinned for the first time in many days as his family enveloped him in a warm embrace. In that mass of bodies, glued to each other with affection, he felt his being down to the smallest atom. He saw the heads sticking out like black woolen balls, some with his trademark curly hair, others bearing Mata ji's brownish sleek tresses. Yes. This was his gene pool.

In that moment, he understood how the mighty banyan in his garden felt, as it's roots grew further away and spawned new saplings, distanced yet inextricably linked to it, the same sap flowing through their veins—a mole here, a finger slightly bent there, the curve of the cheek, the hook of the nose, tiny infirmities secretly carried within the blood stream and passed on from generation to generation.

In their comforting warmth, he saw his life pass before his eyes, toiling with Mata ji to raise this brood, their transformation from toddlers and wailing infants to independent men and women. He felt a deep sense of satisfaction.

'Mata ji did a great job in bringing you up. She would be proud to see you today,' Pandit ji smiled pensively. 'So, what do you wise kids suggest we do now?'

'Let's hold a *dasva* for Mata ji tomorrow. Followed by a *terahvin*. She lived a full life, one that deserves celebration and rememberance, I'll send out the news and invite everyone,' Sudheer took charge. He knew that his outwardly stonehearted father was a disaster at planning any event.

Pandit ji's grateful smile confirmed it.

'I'll take care of the gifts for the guests. Steel glasses engraved with Mata ji's name along with clothes should be a good parting gift. What do you think?' Anu pitched in.

'That sounds perfect,' Chhaya announced with murmurs of approval from the others.

'I'll be Master Chef along with Gauri and Chedilal. Is that all right, Badi Bhabhi?' Indu remarked tongue-in-cheek and a roar of laughter arose from the gathering.

'And I? What should I do?' a tiny voice called out. It was Rani, Anu's youngest daughter. She gazed at her mother with a solemn expression.

Varsha swept her into her arms.

'How could we forget to give you some chore, Rani? You shall look after the most important person in the house—Pandit ji. You are not to leave him alone even for a minute. You can read with him, play ludo, monopoly or cards. Is that all right?'

Rani nodded with such gusto and determination that laughter broke out again.

'Order is called, please,' Randheer assumed the manner of a court bailiff. 'Thank you. With universal consent, the tasks are assigned as follows: Sumit Bhaiyya, Varsha and I shall spread the word in the court, Sudheer shall take care of the others;

Indu Bhabhi and Anu shall make all the arrangements; as usual, Chhaya Bhabhi shall supervise everybody and Madhu shall try and keep out of others' way!'

'You cannot imagine how much I have missed the sound of laughter in this Haveli, Chedi Bhaiyya,' Gauri remarked as she dabbed at her eyes with her dupatta.

'Indeed. I wish Mata ji were around to see them together like this…'

***

Night lingered in the Haveli, making its way slowly from room to room, prolonging its journey, clinging with wispy fingers, loath to leave yet unable to stay. Thoughts floated like clouds, flitting in and out of minds. Words struggled to form fully, some were stifled, others were uttered prematurely.

For the restless individuals occupying it, the Haveli provided the tranquility of a sanctuary. Was it because a piece of their soul was embedded in its stone and masonry structure? Conversely, was a piece of the building lodged deep in their psyche? After decades, it still felt like 'home', to lie in the rooms where they had laughed and cried, fought and made up.

Something buried deep within the Haveli was calling out to them, like a musical instrument whose sound reverberates in others of its ilk. It was alive, an imperious master, summoning their spirits to do its bidding.

The tug on the subconscious was irresistible. Little by little, one by one, each person responded to the diktat.

***

'Thank God, the meeting in the afternoon went well. I was a bit apprehensive.'

'Same here, Sudheer. Somehow, it was a relief when Pandit ji agreed to face the truth.'

'Is it the truth, Randheer? Will we discover what happened to Mata ji?'

'I don't know. But, it was a big load off my head when Pandit ji agreed to perform the rituals tomorrow.'

There was a companionable silence as the two brothers sat in the darkened verandah after dinner. The other members of the family had retired for the day. A lone bulb flickered in the distance, near the gate, emitting weak flashes of light randomly.

'It's like the old times, when all of us used to stay together.'

'Hmm. Why did you move out, Randheer? You never told me.'

'Because you never asked!'

'Well, I am now. Asking, I mean.'

They chuckled.

The still darkness engulfed them again.

'I'm waiting, Randheer.'

There was a sudden flash of yellow light from the bulb. It burnt brightly and then went out with a suddenness that reeked of finality.

Someone sighed in the darkness.

Both Sudheer and Randheer stirred uneasily.

'Did you hear that?'

'I thought it was you sighing like a furnace!'

'Now is not the time to get romantic, my dear bard. I can't see anything. It's so dark. Let's go inside.'

'Not so quickly, old man. I am not moving till you answer me.'

'You always were a persistent pest, Sudheer. How does the army put up with you?'

'I refuse to get side tracked. Are you opening up or...'

'There isn't much to tell, frankly. It was Varsha's idea. After you left, the rest of us started feeling restive. We wanted to be on our own, to live on our terms, chasing *our* dreams without someone throwing disapproving glances at us, without the words of censure that we thought were being uttered behind our backs.'

'You don't sound too sure of your decision.' Sudheer asked gently in the pause that ensued.

'I'm not. I think it was one of the worst decisions I made. For one, the expenses went up astronomically. Varsha started legal practice and for a while we did well. But our measly salary could not support the lavish lifestyle we aspired to. The children were growing up. School fees, extra classes and books had to be paid for. We kept a maid because often Varsha would get delayed at work. Each month when I sat down to balance my accounts like Shyamlal, I was in the red, Sudheer.'

'I wondered,' Sudheer murmured softly, 'why you would leave everything that destiny bestowed with such kindness on you. I did not have a choice. My job in the army did not permit me the luxury of living in my house, with my parents. But you, you had everything laid out before you to pick from. Yet, you disregarded it.'

'The grass is always greener... We envied you—your cantonment bungalow, the glamour and the club parties.'

They laughed without humour, almost tragically.

'Have you ever thought...'

'Thousands of times. I've rehearsed the lines but lacked the courage to say them to Mata ji. Our departure distressed her greatly.'

'You were her favourite, after all!'

'I guess so. In the last few years, she got along fairly well with Varsha too. Perhaps something to do with Varsha being out of the house most of the time! They would sit in this verandah after dinner and chat for hours. Varsha found an eager listener in Mata ji who lapped up the gossip from the court.'

'Then why?'

Randheer shook his head perplexedly.

'I don't know. A whim, maybe. For which we have paid a heavy price, as Varsha now realises only too well.'

'It is not the end of the world, Randheer. Why don't you move back in? You live in a rented house, isn't it?' Sudheer grew excited, the idea taking shape even as he spoke. 'Yes, that would be for the best. Pandit ji would draw enormous strength from your presence. He is fond of Varsha and the children. Why don't you ask Varsha?'

'Do you think Pandit ji will forget the past and take us back?'

'You talk like a complete nincompoop at times, Randheer! Makes me wonder how you are a successful lawyer,' Sudheer laughed. 'Your returning to the Haveli will be a gift to Pandit ji.'

Randheer's face lit up in the dark. His smile glowed.

'There. It's decided. Go and convince Varsha.'

Sudheer continued to sit alone after an animated Randheer left. He gazed out at the lawns, the sweeping branches of the parijat and took deep breaths of the sweet scent of the raat-kirani. One day, when he was free from the bonds of profession, he would come here and—

'Are you planning to stay here the whole night?'

'Oh! I did not hear you come, Indu.'

Indu sat down on the chair still warm from Randheer's body.

'How was the tête-à-tête between the brothers?'

'The usual.'

'Did he agree to shift back to the Haveli?'

'Yes—Wait! How did you know?' Sudheer sat up in his chair.

Indu's laughter tinkled like moonlight in the darkness.

'I'm clairvoyant,' she replied playfully.

A few moments passed with both of them lost in their own thoughts. Then Indu spoke up.

'They seem to have gone through a rough patch. What with Varsha attending the court full-time, juggling the house and her work must have been stressful. Varsha has talked of little else in the last few days. I'm glad for them. Guddu and Mitu will enjoy coming back to the Haveli and the dogs.'

Sudheer nodded silently. There was not much he could tell his perspicacious wife. Thus, when the softly worded request came, it caught him off-guard.

'Can I ask you something?'

'Hmm.'

'When you retire, is it necessary for us to also come back to the Haveli?'

'Of course! Where else will we go?'

'I was wondering if…'

'Is it that you don't want to come back?'

'Not really,' Indu twisted the end of her sari around her finger and stopped when she realised it betrayed her nervousness.

Then, with the suddenness of glass shattering, she blurted out, 'Actually, yes!'

Once the initial ambivalence was overcome, she rushed on, 'Don't misunderstand me. I'm extremely attached to Pandit ji. And the others too. But nothing much has changed in this Haveli. Madhu continues to be vain and irresponsible, Chhaya and Varsha Bhabhi full of guile, and for Anu and Sumi didi it is the sanctuary where they assume their roles of impetuous young women.'

There was a pause. Perhaps Indu was out of breath. Perhaps she wanted to gauge her husband's reaction. There was none. After some time, she continued.

'They have not changed, and neither have we. But like well-worn shoes, the rough edges have been smoothened so that the foot fits better; the angularities accommodated and even celebrated. I guess this is the beauty of life—all of us are different and our distinctions make us complete. With time, I have come to love them, but that does not blind me to their flaws. Neither does it lessen my resolve to lead my life independently.

Familiarity breeds contempt. I understand it better than most people. I would prefer to have a relationship sweetened by distance and not tainted by presumptuousness. I do not know if this makes any sense…'

There was no response.

Indu sighed deeply.

'Well, there is a long day ahead of us. Good night.'

For the second time that night, Sudheer stared out at the moonlit vista. His lips twisted into a travesty of a smile.

'O Destiny! You picked the wrong man,' he mocked himself.

And then he started sobbing uncontrollably, releasing the bottled-up pain and tension.

***

In the room that they had occupied as young girls in the Haveli, Vinu whispered, 'Have you slept, Sumi?'

'No, dear. Ever since Anil ji passed away, I have difficulty sleeping at night.'

'Being alone must be terrible.'

'I've got used to it now, Vinu. And Mummy ji is there. She is now close to eighty. We spend a lot of time together, going to the temple or attending the akhand pāth. It becomes very taxing for her when I'm not there. In fact, that is the reason I was unable to come to Aamnagri despite Mata ji's repeated invitations for the last three years. There was no one who would care for Mummy ji in my absence. Fortunately, Anilji's sister agreed to come over and take her for a few days when I came here. If I had known that Mata ji would react in this manner I would have come under any circum— What happened Vinu? Why are you crying?'

Vinu's body was wracked with sobs.

'I am to blame for this mess, Sumi. No, no, let me finish, please. Mata ji called me a day before she disappeared. She was pleading with me to come over for a few days. I refused. And then I fought with her and banged the phone. She must have been devastated.'

Vinu dissolved into an uncontrollable bout of tears. Sumi tried to console her but without much success.

Vinu continued, her hiccups loudly echoing in the room, 'I spoke to Dinesh yesterday. I've bungled everything and I'll have to do something to set it right. I'm moving back to Aamnagri. Sonu already has a job. Monu can continue his coaching here. Last month, Dinesh was offered a job in the new Medical College that has come up here. Initially he refused. After this tragedy, for my sake, he is reconsidering the offer.'

'Oh! That's incredible!' Sumi hugged her younger sister affectionately. 'Have you told Pandit ji? He will be thrilled.'

Vinu shook her head.

'Will he Sumi? Won't he blame me for this fiasco? I won't be surprised if he doesn't want to see my face again.'

'Don't be thick headed,' Sumi admonished. 'I'm certain, he will be thrilled to know that you will be around. Where will you stay? Wait! Why don't you move into the Haveli?' Sumi gushed excitedly as she saw things falling into place. 'You could provide the much-needed companionship to Pandit ji. You would be doing the rest of us a favour—with you around, we would not have to worry about his well-being.'

Vinu looked at her sister with relief evident on her face. Sumi's advice was music to her ears. She softly confessed, 'I would love to! It would alleviate some of the guilt that I am cursed to carry for the rest of my life.'

There was silence as the sisters reflected on the past. Then Vinu shook herself out of her reverie, 'In case that does not work out, Dinesh has been offered accommodation within the campus of the Medical College. It is not too far away and I can keep an eye on Pandit ji. But I'm worried about Pandit ji's response. Will he…'

Sumi embraced her younger sister warmly.

'You are a perpetual worrier! Leave it to me. I'll handle Pandit ji. I'm so happy that you are doing this, Vinu.' Then she remarked wistfully, 'You are fortunate to have a husband as supportive as Dinesh.'

'Oh Sumi! You must be missing Jija ji. Why don't you shift to Aamnagri, too? No, no. I am serious. Give it a thought. After all, it is only you and Mummy ji, what with Neha and Manu being on their own. And it is not as if you are living in your own house. How long do you want to continue in a rented place? You could always live with us, or in the Haveli. I'm sure, Pandit ji will be happier to have you around than me.'

Now it was Sumi's turn to mull over her sister's counsel.

'It *would* take care of a lot of things. Mummy ji does not like the new landlord. We've lived in that house on rent for the last thirty-five years. The Kapoors were wonderful people and we were extremely close-knit. The new family, regrettably, are poles apart. Sometimes I feel that their abominable behaviour is partly to get rid of us.'

'Doesn't Mummy ji have family in Aamnagri? If you move here, she can be closer to them.' Vinu clapped her hands in delight. 'Oh! This is proving to be so much fun. All of us together. Come on Sumi! Promise me you will move here, please.'

'Arrey! Hold your horses! I need to discuss it with Manu, Neha and Mummy ji first. If they agree, then I need to seek Pandit ji's permission.'

'To quote you: 'Leave it to me. I'll handle Pandit ji.''

Sumi looked at the supine figure of her youngest sister, who slept, oblivious to the happenings around her, 'Should we wake up Anu and break the good news to her?'

Vinu shook her head.

'She has been on her feet the entire day, what with the gifts being bought and wrapped. Let her rest. As it is, we need to ascertain Pandit ji's response first. No point counting your chickens before they hatch.'

***

'Didi! Didi!' Lakshmi's voice was insistent and charged with terror. When Gauri did not reply, she shook her with renewed vigour. 'Wake up, Didi!'

Gauri opened eyes bleary with sleep. She was not too amused at being shaken awake in the middle of the night.

'What is it, Lakshmi? I'm exhausted. Can't it wait till morning?'

'I saw Mata ji's ghost, Didi!'

'What gibberish is this? Have you taken leave of your senses? Go back to sleep. We have work to do tomorrow, young lady.'

'But, Didi—'

'No ifs or buts. I'm *not* going to be kept awake in the night because you have a hyperactive imagination,' Gauri rolled over, away from Lakshmi's dejected puppy-like countenance and tried to regain soporific comfort. 'I should not have consented to having her sleep in my room. Young girls! Full of fanciful visions.'

For some time, Gauri's regular breathing was the only sound in the small staff quarter. A chastised Lakshmi stared at the ceiling as she tried to find the elusive sleep. She turned restlessly from side to side. The old bed creaked loudly each time she moved.

'Okay,' Gauri remarked exasperatedly as she turned back to face Lakshmi. 'Tell me what is bothering you. But it better be a good reason or I'll skin you alive.'

Lakshmi sat up ebulliently. Her smile competed with the fear lurking in the depths of her eyes.

'I've been meaning to tell you for a few days but I was scared you wouldn't believe me. But you must trust me. Do you promise? I swear Mata ji's ghost is roaming around in the Haveli.' When Gauri looked like she would smack her in irritation, Lakshmi cut straight to the point.

'Remember, you sent me to the outhouse the other day to fetch the dry mangoes? Gangu Bhaiyya stores them there. Well, when I reached there, I saw Mata ji's neatly folded sari lying on the bed. And her slippers under it.'

'Spooks don't keep saris and slippers, Lakshmi,' Gauri observed wryly. 'In all probability the slippers belong to Gangu Bhaiyya. He must have left them there when he went to his village last month. The sari could be an old one, used by him to cover plants or for drying stuff.'

'Maybe. So I went back the next day to the outhouse to check. The things were missing. Instead, the bed looked freshly made and someone had used the bathroom. There was water on the floor and in the bucket. Gangu bhaiyya is not around, so who is living in the outhouse? I'm sure it is none other than Mata ji's ghost.'

Gauri looked as if she was running out of patience. Lakshmi hastily came to what she thought was the clincher.

'When I went there today, I found Mata ji's tulsi beads kept on the table near the window. Inside, the room was spick and span. It was far cleaner than I've ever seen it. The door was locked from outside.' And then, in the manner of a conjurer pulling the rabbit out of the hat, Lakshmi announced, 'The smell of incense was all around—Mata ji's favourite, *chandan agarbatti*. The same ones she bought last month and lit in the temple every morning.'

'Hmmm. Something is amiss. Why didn't you tell me this earlier?'

'Because Gauri didi, you are extremely patient and open-minded, not a wee bit intimidating,' Lakshmi's precocious observation earned her a chuckle from Gauri.

'Okay, Ms Karamchand. Tomorrow morning, we shall visit the outhouse to find out who is using Mata ji's valuable *chandan agarbatti*.'

***

Mornings in Aamnagri were unique. The breeze was cool, wafting the scent of mango blossoms in the early part of the year or the earthy fragrance of wet earth during the monsoons. The sun was radiant, glowing like an ember amidst the invigorating iciness of pearl-white clouds. And the chirping of birds, in perfect harmony with the chiming temple bells, interspersed with the stillness of silence, played out like a well-orchestrated performance. Gauri and Lakshmi rose at their regular hour and quickly headed towards the outhouse. They were armed with a stick each to tackle the intruder.

'See, Didi. The door is not latched. I distinctly remember closing it yesterday.'

'Shhh! We must not give our presence away. Otherwise the thief will escape.'

They carefully inched open the door.

The room was bare.

Gauri's eyes swept over the items inside. A bed, covered with an old sheet. A wooden chair in the corner. A ramshackle wooden cupboard with its door coming off the hinges.

No sari. No slippers. No agarbatti.

'You wretch! So much for your detective skills. Dragged me to this place for nothing. The work that we have to do, and look at us, rummaging about in empty outhouses when we should have been neck deep in work in the kitchen. Run along! You shall have the honours of cleaning the pots and pans today,' Gauri finished viciously.

***

'Come inside for a moment, please,' Chhaya pulled Sumeet into their old bedroom, away from prying eyes and ears.

'Is everything all right?'

'It depends on what you call all right.'

Sumeet looked at his wife exasperatedly. She enjoyed speaking in riddles. Well, he had got used to it by now. Like an experienced fisherman, he patiently waited for the fish to bite.

'I presume you think it is splendid news that your younger brother and two sisters are shifting back into the Haveli.'

'Of course. It takes a big load off my head to not worry about Pandit ji living alone in this oversized house. I could sense Vinu's insecurity when she broached the matter with Pandit ji at the breakfast table. Or rather when Sumi mentioned it in passing. But Pandit ji's answer allayed our fears. His joy knew no bounds. In fact, his pleasure made me…'

'Yes?' Chhaya prompted softly.

'It made me feel homesick. Memories of our times together in this house came rushing back. If only…'

'Yes, Sumeet,' Chhaya prodded impatiently. 'If only what?'

'Do you think… Is it possible for you to consider… I mean, can we come back here?'

'I thought you'd never ask, you dense, foolish man!' Chhaya flung her arms around Sumeet. 'Ever since their announcement this morning, I've been sick with worry. If we do not return to the Haveli, who knows what will happen to our share in the property. Yes, yes. You are outraged. But then, you have never been petty-minded like your siblings. We have to keep an eye over them and save what is rightfully ours.

Leave it to me. At a suitable time we, too, shall proclaim our filial love and consequent desire to return to the Haveli.

And wipe off that expression of appalled horror before we join the others.'

With that she gave a small push to Sumeet that propelled him out of the room into the hall. From the doorway of her old room, she looked back. Determination was writ large on her face.

'No one will take my place here. No one.'

***

At the lunch table, the dourness of the morning was replaced by a sense of expectation. The terahvin ceremony was to be conducted in the evening.

'You are unbelievable, Indu Bhabhi! With your talent for organisation, you should have pursued a career as an event manager. They are the latest fad in all weddings and birthdays,' Vinu exclaimed.

Indu smiled at the compliment. Vinu looked ten years younger after receiving Pandit ji's consent to shift into the Haveli.

'If you have finished admiring Indu Bhabhi's handiwork, perhaps you would take a moment to appreciate the gifts,' Anu chimed in.

'Waah! Waah!'

'Maashallah!'

'Super work, Anu.'

'Thank you, thank you. We are all set for the big event this evening. The guests—'

'Before you launch into details of the evening programme,' Chhaya interjected, 'I want to make an announcement.'

All eyes turned towards Chhaya and Sumeet. Pandit ji slipped his moon-shaped spectacles down his nose and peered over them.

'Well, well, well,' he muttered under his breath. 'The day's bombshells are not over. Another surprise declaration!'

To his utter disbelief, Sumeet came over and touched his feet. Pandit ji could scarcely mask his astonishment. The boy had not sought his benediction since he passed his Bar Council exams.

'*Khush raho*! *Khush raho*! What is all this about?'

'Pandit ji, we want to come back to be with you.'

Anu let out a whoop of delight. The others started clapping. Sumi hugged Chhaya.

'Yes, Pandit ji,' Chhaya extricated herself from the choking embrace with difficulty. 'If you will have us, that is.'

Pandit ji burst out laughing at her mournful and contrite expression. Then realising the inappropriateness of his reaction, he quickly took off his glasses and began to polish them.

'This is your home,' he replied. 'You do not need my permission to come here. As a father, the doors of my house have always been and shall always remain open for my children.'

Amidst the loud laughter and cheering that followed Pandit ji's wise words, the old man slipped away to his office.

'You left your door open as promised, Pandit ji.'

'Oh! It's you, Indu. Come inside. I hope there are no more bolts from the blue for me. I am getting on in age and would prefer a more sedate life,' Pandit ji laughed mirthlessly.

Indu walked around the room wordlessly, tracing the leather-bound volumes of legal treatises that occupied shelves stretching from the ceiling to the floor.

'No. I have no intention of delivering a googly, Pandit ji,' she replied after a few minutes, 'though there may be others planning to.'

Pandit ji's eyebrows rose enquiringly.

Indu shrugged and continued, 'Nothing very tangible, as yet. But Vineet and Madhu mentioned an offer to work in Aamnagri.'

Pandit ji nodded. He wondered what had drawn Indu into his office for this discussion. She was not one to make small talk.

'You are not happy with the birds flying back into the nest, Pandit ji. Why is that?'

Pandit ji let out a full-throated laugh.

'Cross-questioning me, is it? When I was speculating on the reasons for your coming here, little did I expect that it was to put me in the witness box. Not that it matters. In fact, it will be a relief to share my thoughts with someone. I hope you will not misunderstand my melancholy. I am overjoyed that one by one, all my children want to come and live with me. Most of them are doing it out of affection. The rest…' Pandit ji shrugged philosophically. 'My regret is that their decision comes a bit late. If only…'

'If only? If only what, Pandit ji?'

Pandit ji shook his head ruefully. He could not bring himself to articulate the thoughts churning within.

Indu looked as if she would press him further. Then she checked herself. A shadow of acute disappointment passed over her face.

Without another word, she left.

***

It was late evening by the time the last guest departed. The scent of Mata ji's favourite incense lingered in the Haveli. Her black and white photograph, adorned with a garland of rose petals, sat on a chair in the drawing room. Crisp white sheets, spread out for the guests to seat themselves, lay mussed and soiled. The Awasthi clan occupied different places in the room, emotionally drained and feeling much like the limpid bed sheets.

For a long time, no one spoke. Words seemed pointless. The terahvin ceremony had an air of finality about it, a closure to a life and its associations. Mata ji was gone. There was no returning. Those left behind would have to move on without her presence in this world.

Pandit ji roused himself with an effort and managed a feeble smile.

'A job well done. Mata ji would be proud of your work if she were watching from above. Let us call it a day.'

As the others shuffled to their feet, Indu interjected, 'Wait! Chhote Mama is yet to come.'

'I don't think he is coming, Indu,' Randheer commented.

'He would not if he has any self respect.'

'I agree. How could he and Mami impute Mata ji's disappearance to any negligence on Pandit ji's part? As if she was a young girl who lost her way.'

'Hardly! If anyone is to be held accountable for this fiasco, it is Mata ji.'

'Madhu, keep quiet!' Vineet hissed.

'No, Vineet. Let me speak. For the last few days, we have been talking about Mata ji as a paragon of virtue, a goddess above reproach. Nothing could be further from the truth. She was an unpleasant person in life. The ignominy she has wrought upon us by her mysterios disappearance is something none of us is likely to forget,' Madhu paused for breath.

'She is right,' Chhaya sniffed. 'Mrs Tiwari gave me a long sermon on daughters-in-law. Ufff! My ears are still burning with her rebukes.'

'Stop!' Pandit ji's voice was like silk, its deceptive softness masking the inherent sharpness. 'Stop it both of you. Do you realise what you are saying?

Shakuntala did not ask you to edify her. She made no claims of being a saint. All she desired was to have her children close to her. Did you know that at one time she harboured dreams of becoming a college professor? Unfortunately, her love for her children was stronger. If she had pursued her ambitions, who knows, she would have been with us today. She forfeited a promising career and hobbies to raise you.

She invested all her time in you. And then, one by one, each of you left. It shattered her. Though you did not look back to check on your mother, she never stopped looking out for you. When you set up homes and built lives away from the Haveli, it was as if you were sucking out the oxygen from her home. Day by day she grew emaciated, deprived of the sound of your voices and laughter.

But you are not culpable. You did what every ordinary human being does. You did it without mens rea.

I am the true perpetrator. I, who knew what tortured her soul, who had sworn to be by her side through thick and thin, through the good times and the bad, it is I who am squarely responsible. If you wish to vilify someone for this disaster, Madhu and Chhaya, point towards me. Shakuntala suffered enough during her lifetime. I implore you to spare her after her death.

There! I've said it. She is DEAD. And I am her executioner.'

Pandit ji's voice cracked as he uttered these terrible words. He hid his face in his hands and his body shuddered. Madhu and Chhaya shrank back in horror.

The past few days, they had assiduously avoided mentioning death. Partly to spare Pandit ji's feelings, partly to deny the truth staring at them. Now, there was no escaping it.

'I agree with you, Pandit ji.'

The gathering turned around in disbelief to find Chhote Mama standing at the threshold.

'You heard me correctly. Indeed, it is you who killed my sister. However, you are fortunate to receive an opportunity to atone for your crime.'

'It can't be possible...' Pandit ji half rose from his chair then fell back disconsolately. 'Don't mock a ruined man, Ashok.'

Chhote Mama smiled. Without a word he moved aside to reveal the shadowy figure tucked behind him.

'Shakuntala!'

All the misery, hopelessness and despair of the past few days broke free from Pandit ji. He rushed forward like a school boy who has found his prized possession. One that he thought was lost forever.

'Oh Shakuntala! Is it really you? Where did you go away?'

Before anyone could react, little Lakshmi flew across the room and floored Mata ji with a deadly tackle.

'Here! I've trapped the evil spirit. Quick! Gauri didi, bring the rope to tie her up,' Lakshmi huffed as she sat atop the squirming figure.

The others were immobilised with fear and shock. They gaped at the bizarre scene unfolding before their eyes.

'Gauri didi! Why aren't you doing as I'm telling you. I can't keep it down forev—'

'Help! Pandit ji, help me!' spluttering and gasping for breath, Mata ji dislodged Lakshmi and sat up.

'Lakshmi, you nutcase, let go of her!' Pandit ji dashed towards the two entangled and wrestling bodies. With great tenderness, he lifted Mata ji off the floor and led her to a comfortable sofa.

The rest of the family stared dumbfounded at this unbelievable reunion. It was beyond anything they had imagined in their wildest dreams.

After a brief pause, thrilled cries of 'Mata ji! You are back!' rent the air. Gauri and Chedilal fell at Mata ji's feet and refused to let go, almost lifting her off the ground. In hapless surrender, Mata ji slumped onto the sofa and was promptly surrounded by her family who were talking nineteen to the dozen. Chhote Mama and Indu observed the happenings from a distance.

'It worked. A chance remark by Madhu and Badi Bhabhi did the trick.'

'I was beginning to lose hope, Indu. He is a stubborn man, our Pandit ji. I thought he would never acknowledge Didi's worth and she would have to fade away from his life. She was determined to do so unless she heard it in as many words from him.'

'Last evening, I felt he was on the verge of saying so. On my suggestion, Mata ji waited in the anteroom next to his office. I tried to provoke him into an admission of remorse. When he did not, she was broken,' Indu shook her head regretfully.

'It was a close call even at this stage. Didi was insistent that unless Pandit ji spelt it out in black and white, she would not come back. She preferred to take sanyas rather than lead a life of humiliation and indifference. Did you know that she had made up her mind to spend her remaining days in Guru ji's ashram in Rishikesh? She seemed to be looking forward to a life of solitude. All these days, while she hid herself in Gangu Mali's quarters, she spent her time meditating, almost like a hermit in *samadhi*. I was not aware of this deeply spiritual side to Didi's personality. It is Guru ji's kripa that things have turned out the way we wished,' Chhote Mama sighed.

Indu nodded in agreement.

'Let us hope that the threads of attachment are strong enough to keep her with us.'

'Rest assured, Indu,' Chhote Mama chuckled. 'Pandit ji is not a man to make the same mistake twice. My sister will find herself a prisoner of love.'

Six months later...

'Gauri, don't prepare any dinner tonight.'

'Why, Badi Bhabhi?'

'Arrey! Today is Saturday.'

'So?'

'Uff-o! Do I have to spell out everything loudly? Today is Saturday. Pandit ji and Mata ji are going for the bridge party. The rest of us are going out to celebrate Varsha's appointment as the Standing Counsel for the Aamnagri Bar.'

'Are you sure? Sumi didi mentioned that I should prepare something light for her tonight.'

'I am sure, dear. We decided last week and most likely it has slipped her mind. Now off you go to watch some TV.'

'Where is Gauri being sent?' Mata ji stepped into the kitchen.

'I was asking her to take the evening off. We are planning to celebrate Varsha's promotion tonight.'

'Of course! I hope you enjoy yourself.'

'Thank you, Mata ji. Where is your bridge party this week?'

'Where else but Dr Saxena's house? Ever since I lent Guru ji's latest book to Mrs Saxena, she has taken a fancy to me. A most hospitable and warm personality, I must admit. Keeps saying that we should have met earlier. Can you imagine? Pandit ji and Mr Saxena have been friends for several decades but the two of us did not know we had so much in common. Last time we spent an hour discussing the chapter on judging people and forming impressions without knowing the whole truth. Guru ji has discussed this extensively in his first book.'

Chhaya nodded blindly. She had no clue what Mata ji was referring to, but she played along.

'I used to detest Pandit ji's bridge parties. Primarily because I felt left out while he enjoyed himself over dinner and drinks with his friends. How imprudent I was not to have joined him earlier!'

As Mata ji fell silent, lost in her thoughts, Chhaya pitched in.

'How are your bridge lessons coming along?'

'Eh? Bridge? Simply wonderful,' Mata ji's face split into a grin. 'Pandit ji and I won all the rubbers last week.'

'That is amazing. Must be beginner's luck,' the words were out of her mouth before Chhaya could stop, 'or perhaps you have inherent talent,' she finished lamely.

'Neither, my dear,' Mata ji patted her hand kindly. 'It's all about vastushastra.'

'Vastushastra? What has that got to do with your winnings at the bridge table?'

'Everything, darling. When you reach my age, you will discover that events in life have a purpose. The sooner we acknowledge and accept it, the more advantageous it is for us.' Chhaya was flummoxed by this philosophical discourse.

Seeing that her daughter-in-law had no clue what she was referring to, Mata ji kindly elaborated, 'Do you remember the ornately carved wall mirror that I gifted Mrs Saxena last month?'

'Hmmm,' Chhaya acquiesced mutely. She was having trouble keeping up with Mata ji's blistering change of thought. 'The one Malati mami brought for you? I remember you said it wouldn't fit in with the decor of the Haveli.'

'The same one. I thought it was perfect for the Saxena's drawing room. So, I took it along the last time they hosted us for dinner. As luck would have it, Mrs Saxena fell in love with it at first sight. It occupies a place of pride in her drawing room. Incidentally, the bridge table is kept right in front of it,' Mata ji paused for effect, and to allow Chhaya to piece the puzzle together.

When Chhaya continued to stare at her in bafflement, she sighed and remarked, 'I have been fortuitous to be seated facing the mirror while Pandit ji sits in front of me.'

She pretended to develop a sudden interest in the paisley pattern on the ceramic teapot as she waited for Chhaya to figure it out.

Chhaya gasped in disbelief, 'Haven't the others realised what is happening?'

Mata ji continued her examination of the teapot.

'One is, of course, extremely discreet and cautious. It helps that the room is not too well-lit. Mrs Saxena is convinced that muted illumination is a hallmark of sophistication. On the whole, these Saturday gatherings are proving to be a lucrative affair. Pandit ji is pleased as punch. He loses no opportunity to take credit for—'

'Shakuntala! Shakuntala! Where are you? It's time to leave.'

Mata ji's face lit up. She smiled like a young girl off on her first date.

Chhaya could not hold back her answering smile. This woman had rediscovered her zest for life. She gently pushed Mata ji towards the exit.

'I'm so glad you went away, Mata ji. Pandit ji found his Shakuntala again...'

Glossary

Achkan: Long jacket for men. Long button-down coat worn on formal occasions.

Amavasya: Moonless night

Arti: Religious ceremony involving praying with lit lamps and ringing bells.

Bhabhi: Wife of elder brother.

Bhrigu Samhitā: An astrological (Jyotish) classic attributed to Maharishi Bhrigu during the Vedic period which is believed to predict the past, present and future of an individual.

Chaat: A spicy, fried snack.

Chabuk: Whip

Chachi: Aunt

Chhutti: Vacations

Dadi: Paternal grandmother

Dasva: Ceremony held on the tenth day after death where offerings and donation are made to ensure that the soul rests in peace.

Dehri: Threshold.

Dhobi: Washerman

Gangajal: Water of the River Ganges, considered sacred and capable of purifying everything it comes in contact with.

Gujiya: Fried dumpling stuffed with a sweet mixture.

Jethani: Sister-in-law

Kaddu Ki Sabzi: A dish prepared by using pumpkin.

Kony: Assamese word for egg.

Kudi: Girl

Mali: Gardener.

Mangalsutra: Black beaded necklace worn by married women as a sign of matrimony.

Mutt: A place where religious men, saints and ascetics live. Often it is attached to a temple.

Ojha: An exorcist

Parijat: Indian night jasmine

Samadhi: State of meditative consciousness.

Shikhandi: Reference to the character Shikhandi in Mahabharat who is responsible for Bhishma's defeat.

Tabeez: Amulet, protective charm

Taiji: Aunt

Teekhi mirchi: Red-hot chilly

Terahvin: Prayer meeting held on the thirteenth day after a person's death. It is believed that on this day, the soul begins its journey to the world beyond. Marks a point of no return.

Themis: Goddess of Justice and Divine law in ancient Greece

Videshi: literally means foreigners and refers to those coming from outside the country.

Yoga Danda: Y shaped wooden stick used by saints to rest their arm while clicking their beads.

Born and brought up in Lucknow, **Shubha Sarma** is an alumnus of Lady Shri Ram College and Jawaharlal Nehru University and a member of the Indian Administrative Service. A Yoga practitioner, she enjoys travelling, swimming and tending to her bonsai collection. She currently lives in Bhubaneswar with her husband, two sons and four dogs.

Her debut book *Fly on the Wall & Other Stories* was launched in 2013 and was translated into Hindi and Italian. It received rave reviews from readers and critics alike. Her body of work displays strong characters and reflects the changing times that confront us. This is her second novel.

Shubha_Sarma@twitter.com